Lady Duffus Hardy

In Sight of Land

A Novel: Vol. II.

Lady Duffus Hardy

In Sight of Land
A Novel: Vol. II.

ISBN/EAN: 9783337065065

Printed in Europe, USA, Canada, Australia, Japan

Cover: Foto ©Andreas Hilbeck / pixelio.de

More available books at **www.hansebooks.com**

IN SIGHT OF LAND.

A NOVEL.

BY

LADY DUFFUS HARDY,

AUTHOR OF "BERYL FORTESCUE," &c.

IN THREE VOLUMES.

VOL. II.

London:

WARD AND DOWNEY,

12, YORK STREET, COVENT GARDEN.

1885.

CONTENTS.

CONTENTS.

CHAPTER XI.

BREAKERS AHEAD!

THE fair dove of peace had folded its wings, and sat brooding and cooing above the old grey Manor House for six whole weeks; no adverse breeze had blown to make it flutter its wings and fly. Full ripe summer had come, and was flaunting in all its glory of fruits and flowers, soft airs and brilliant sunshine. Little sociabilities had been carried on, hospitalities given and received, throughout the scattered society of Penally and its neighbourhood; each party paid back its debts to the other, paid back its dinners and luncheons with

scrupulous exactness. A failure in these
social responsibilities was enough to put
anybody in the pillory of public opinion.

A bankrupt in mercantile matters going
through the Common Court of Bankruptcy
has an easy time compared to him who
fails to pay society its dues. Those
Penallyites who failed in their social duties
were written down in their neighbours'
Book of Doom to be quietly ignored next
season, their names fading out as though
written with invisible ink, and gradually
erased from the general visiting-list. Of
course no one spoke plainly on the matter,
and no one dreamed of infringing the laws
of courtesy: but what law can prevent a
woman freezing while she smiles, or being
coldly aggressive in manner while scrupu-
lously polite in words ?

Society in a limited circle is perhaps
more exacting and stands more upon its

dignity, is stronger in its demands and keener in its feelings, than when it has a more extensive and varied growth. There is as much punctiliousness, and the rules of etiquette are as strictly enforced, among the straggling community of this lonely corner of the county, as though it were the great metropolis itself. They arranged their " season," their festivities, kettle-drums and garden parties, strictly on the London plan, all news therefrom being greedily devoured ; and they limped in a poor, pretentious sort of way in the footsteps of the fashionable crowd whirling and re-volving in the distant city. After all, Society means much the same thing to all sorts and conditions of men ; it is human nature holding its revels and exchanging its civilities, sometimes in fustian and common homespun, sometimes in belaced and befrizzled beauty, playing its antics,

and revolving in its own sphere, and about
as real and genuine as the harlequinade in
the Christmas pantomime—but not half so
amusing.

Well, Penally enjoyed itself, as it had a
right to do, according to its own pleasure,
but felt rather aggrieved, if not positively
outraged, by the attitude assumed and
maintained by the family at the Manor
House, who had never extended their
visiting-list beyond the three families with
whom they had made acquaintance on their
first arrival. All civilities and offered hospitalities from other quarters were gracefully
received, but courteously declined, thus in
a general way increasing the hostile feeling
their first coming created; *then* people had
only suspected, *now* they were sure there
was something wrong, and waited till time,
which sooner or later makes all secrets
known, should tell them what.

Meanwhile the absent young men kept up a continual correspondence with their respective families, and all news thus obtained was briskly exchanged through the medium of Clarice Lemaire and Miriam Spencer, for there was generally a message, an inquiry, or some little item of gossip, which the girls thought would be interesting to one another; in fact, the absent ones seemed to be the one link which bound Clarice and Miriam together: in all but the one interest, their sympathies and their natures were as opposite as the antipodes.

One lovely July morning Clarice sat at the head of the breakfast-table, prosaically engaged in pouring out her father's coffee, while he spelt over the latest news from town. A flood of sunlight poured in through the open window and mingled with the golden aureole of her glorious hair, till it seemed to become a part of it, and the

pleasant sea breeze, laden with the perfume of flowers and the song of birds, swept
freely in. The view looking out from the
window was peaceful and lovely in the
extreme : the sea lay at rest in the circling
arms of the shore, its strong heart beating
faintly as its tender wavelets ran in low
rippling laughter along the edge of the
dimpled sand ; a few fishing-smacks with
brown patched sails were floating lazily upon
the water, and the hum of the bees and the
monotonous whirr of the happy insect world
seemed to make the morning drowsy, as
though it would like to shut its eyes and
rest too.

A beautiful picture of still-life it was,
both within and without the house. Clarice,
in the radiant beauty of youth, most flower-
like and fair, was more 'gorgeous than usual
in her colours this morning ; her complexion
was more delicately, brilliantly fair — it

seemed as though the sun's kiss had touched and ripened it to a dainty peach-like bloom; even her deep violet eyes had a gleam of the sunlight in them, as though they had caught the reflected glow from the mass of golden hair which lay coiled like a crown upon her shapely head. She wore a long pale-blue dress trimmed with soft lace, with a knot of yellow roses on her breast. So perfectly harmonious were the colours blended one with the other, she might have sat for a painter's study, "a harmony in gold and blue." Opposite to her, and in grave contrast, sat Mr. Fleming, his good grey head uplifted, his kind eyes resting now and then in tender affection upon her. The usually anxious expression of his face had faded from it; it seemed to have caught the reflection of hers, which at the present moment was calm and untroubled. The agitating emotions which generally disturbed the current of her life, and sent those vague, mysterious waves of light and shadow across her face—and which those who loved her knew so well— were at rest too.

As they sat chatting, he reading aloud any interesting items or scraps of news that came like an echo from the great world of London to them in their seclusion here, a telegram was brought in and delivered to Mr. Fleming. These bits of yellow paper generally bring bad news; that is why they are received always with some trepidation, a sort of shrinking fear. Mr. Fleming glanced through it and put it in his pocket, glancing across the table at Clarice as he did so, and saying—

"Business, my dear, from the Bank."

There was a slight twitching at the corners of his mouth, a gleam of something in his eye, that looked as though the news it

brought was not of an exhilarating kind ;
but of this Clarice took no heed—the simple
words " bank " and " business " satisfied
her. The telegram read thus :

" L. is in London—met him in the
Strand—shall keep an eye upon him."

It would not seem as though this brief
message could mean much to anybody ; but
it meant a great deal to Mr. Fleming. It
disturbed him so much that for the rest of
the meal he relapsed into silence, broken
only when, by fits and starts, he addressed
some wandering words to Clarice, merely
for the sake of saying something, as they
were not *à propos* of anything. Presently
he rose from the table in a preoccupied
kind of way and left the room, just patting
Clarice's head as he passed without saying
a word.

Clarice went through the daily routine,
the superintending of those trifling home

duties which fell to her share. For the house was generally "run" by Katrina, who was a most efficient housekeeper as well as a devoted nurse ; but Clarice liked to feel she had a hand in the domestic arrangements, and when her physical and mental health permitted, was most scrupulous in the discharge of the light fancy duties of her life, which generally lay among the fruits and flowers, conservatory and greenhouses ; then she fed her birds, Jerry and Bouncer looking solemnly on without attempting to molest the feathered favourites, for they knew their time would come ; they watched the lump of sugar, the last token of affection, placed between the bars of the canary's cage, whereon the pretty creature commenced to sing as though it would sing its heart out. Jerry's excitement showed itself from the end of his nose to the tip of his tail, which wagged as though it would wag itself off, his greedy eyes fixed upon the macaroon so temptingly held before him.

"Now, Jerry!" exclaimed his mistress. Jerry knew what was expected of him, and rose up on his hind-legs and gravely turned round three times, then received the biscuit on the end of his nose, threw it up in the air and caught it in his mouth as a conjurer catches his ball; then he received the order to "die," and he stretched himself out and lay down, as though dead of indigestion. Bouncer watched this gymnastic performance with dignified contempt written on his canine countenance, wondering that any well-bred friend of his could condescend to play such tricks. He, however, being only a dog, had his temptations also, though they were of a higher order; he kept his eye upon the silver sugar-bowl—therein lay his temptation and sweet reward.

"Now. Bouncer!" exclaimed his young

mistress, " we will have a little discussion
all to ourselves ; you are a sensible dog
and understand things." Bouncer actually
laughed—dogs *do* laugh, as those who study
their physiognomies know full well—in appreciation of the compliment; and Clarice
proceeded to inquire his opinion of a certain
statesman whose policy was then the general
topic of conversation. Now Jack had been
Bouncer's political trainer, and educated
him on such principles as he deemed most
truly patriotic, and on the mention of the
obnoxious name the British dog showed his
teeth, snarled fiercely, and ended with a
series of low growls, as though he had
swallowed his enemy, who did not sit easy
on his digestion. At the name of the
Prince of Wales he sang, beating an accom-
paniment rhythmically with his tail; and
for Queen Victoria he gave three such joyous
barks they echoed through the house. He

was rewarded by the delicate sweetmeat, which he took from his mistress's hand; the idea of putting it on his nose was an insult not to be thought of—his canine accomplishments were of a higher order than those of his friend and companion.

Clarice then took them both for a scamper through the woods. Glancing across the lawn as she went along, she observed Mr. Fleming pacing slowly up and down between a double row of limes, with his arms folded, his head bowed upon his breast. On her return, in about half an hour, she found him still pacing up and down in precisely the same attitude. She never liked to break in upon his thoughtful moods, but she was tempted to do so now. She tripped lightly across the grass, stood by his side, slipped her hand in his, and walked with him slowly up and down. He took no notice of her movements—indeed seemed even unconscious of her presence; the inquiring look upon her face evoked no answer, but with the same dull brooding on his brow he moved monotonously to and fro. Presently, when she could bear the silence no longer, she said coaxingly—

"Dad, darling, what troubles you? Won't you tell me?"

He stopped then, as though suddenly recalled to himself. Taking her uplifted face between his hands, he kissed her forehead.

"Child, is it so strange that I should enjoy a little stroll alone? Why do you think I am troubled?"

"I don't think, I know; it was that telegram — what was it about? May I see it?"

"Pooh! why should you want to see it? You wouldn't understand."

"But you could explain——"

"There are some things I don't care to

explain or talk about," he answered quickly, as though he disapproved of her questioning. "Life is full of complications, my dear, but we have to struggle through them somehow —somehow. I—I sometimes wish I were well out of it all. If only you were safe and happy, child, I would like to walk straight out of this troublous world this very day."

"You would have to take me with you, then," she answered, nestling closer to him; "I wouldn't stay an hour in the world without you."

"That is nonsense, my child; I shall have to die some day—and I think—it will be soon."

"Don't be so cruel!" exclaimed Clarice, tears starting to her eyes; "if you were to die I think I should die too—it seems impossible that we *can* part for ever and ever with those we love."

" We do not part for ever. It is my firm
faith that we two shall walk together in the
light of a brighter, better world than this,
even as we now walk through this—with
our souls purified, our bodies dust."

" I shouldn't care for that—it wouldn't
be the same thing. It is your very self I
love, the *you* who are here *now*, walking and
talking with me : *there* you will be a mere
voiceless echo of yourself—a poor, chilly,
miserable ghost—a bodiless essence in a
world unknown! I should shrink from you
then, as much as I cling to you now : it is
to the human creature we cling with all our
human love—when that is gone and buried
in the cold earth, all is gone from us. I
should like to feel that when I leave this
world no part of me will ever live again
anywhere."

" We cannot rule these things for ourselves, my dear child. Depend upon it, our

Creator has arranged all things for the best; it is only the worst part, the mere dross of our nature, that perishes here—the better part lives on in a better world."

"I don't know—I don't care about that. It takes two halves to make a whole, and if one part of my nature is here, and another part there, why it wouldn't be *me* at all; I'd as soon be dissolved into nothing at once!"

Mr. Fleming did not care to prolong the conversation, for whenever they drifted into vague speculations they got lost. Besides, he wanted to be alone—Clarice had joined him against his will; and he had a new anxiety upon his mind now, and he wanted to be alone, to put certain *pros* and *cons* side by side and decide what he would do under certain conditions. How fond we all are of doing that—making our plans, what we will say and what we will do, arranging and

dovetailing events and circumstances, fight-
ing our imaginary battles under imaginary
conditions which never occur. We are not
the commanders of fate—the battle opens,
and the conflict takes place on quite a
different ground, and we are forced to face
circumstances we had never contemplated.
Things straighten themselves out without
any aid or guidance of ours, and our air-
built castles are blown down with a breath.

Clarice felt rather than saw that there
was something wrong, but she troubled him
with no more questioning, but vaguely
wondered what the "business" was.

In the afternoon, as she was trying over
some music which Jack had lately sent
down from town, Mr. Fleming came hur-
riedly into the room with a cloth wrapped
about his hand and wrist.

"I have had a little accident, my dear
child, and cut my hand—it is an ugly gash."

"Don't let me see the blood," exclaimed Clarice, hastily, as she rose up shivering and with averted eyes. "You know the sight of blood frightens me."

"It is nothing at all serious, but I think I had better go down to Parkes and have it properly strapped up."

"We'll have the carriage round at once, and I'll go with you," exclaimed Clarice, following her suggestion with prompt action. In a few minutes—that is, as soon as the horses could be put to—the carriage was at the door; Clarice ran down hatted and gloved, and they were off. Fortunately Dr. Parkes was at home, having just returned from his afternoon round; Mr. Fleming accompanied him into the surgery, and his hand was duly examined. "It was an ugly cut," he said, "and had just escaped being a serious one."

Meanwhile, as the Doctor was attending

to her father, Clarice sat chatting with Miss Parkes, the Doctor's maiden sister, who kept his house and looked after his bodily comforts as well as his spiritual welfare; she was rather a tiresome companion, too much given to dwell upon her ailments and on the attractions and triumphs of the days that were gone.

She had once had a profile and a complexion, and could not forget that she had lost both. Though the years had stolen away her charms, and rigorously destroyed every vestige of beauty, both of form and face, she wandered through the realms of art in search of it; she would not be content to bury her dead youth under a cloud of black lace and piety, as some women do. She tried to renovate herself, but she was like a faded old doll that has lost its paint, and no pinching or patching would restore it to its old state.

Not very long had Clarice sat with this lady, rather bored by her twaddling talk, when the genial Doctor and Mr. Fleming reappeared, the wound having been sewn up and properly bandaged. The Doctor was always glad to see Clarice; he regarded her somewhat in the light of a psychological puzzle, and he would have liked to take her to pieces—mentally, not bodily, for he could have made no improvement in her lovely form or face, but if he could have dissected her mind he would have left out some crooked, ill-fitting bits, and put her together again perfect in mind as well as in body. Clarice liked him too, though she rather rebelled against the kind of mesmeric influence he had over her. She did not exactly know what it was, but when she was under his eye she felt compelled to speak when she would rather have been silent, and to say things she would rather

have left unsaid. After a little brief commonplace chat, they were about to take
their departure when old Ben came hobbling
up from the gate ; his errand was brief—
there had been an accident at or rather
near the station, and the Doctor's services
were needed forthwith.

" Jump into my carriage," exclaimed Mr.
Fleming; " we shall be half-way there
before your gig is ready, and time is
precious. Clarice, you will stay with Miss
Parkes ; I will call for you on my return."

He bore away with him a lighter heart
than he would carry again for many a long
day thereafter.

CHAPTER XII.

AN UNWELCOME GUEST.

A T the station all was " confusion worse confounded." About a quarter of a mile before reaching the platform, the axle-bar of the engine had suddenly snapped; it left the rails and went ploughing along the line for some hundred yards, dragging the train of affrighted passengers after it; then it rushed down the slight embankment, the carriages toppling over and crashing after it, the two first carriages being a complete wreck. The hind-part of the train, though swinging and swaying from side to side, had still kept to the rails; the passengers, though terribly shaken, quickly descended to the help of their more unfortunate fellow-travellers, who had been hurled down the embankment with the fore-part of the train, and now lay entangled among the woodwork and splintered fragments of the wrecked carriages. The cries and moans of the wounded men, women, and children were piteous to hear, and the sight was terrible to behold; legs, arms, and bodies being so entangled with the *débris*, it seemed impossible they could be extricated whole and alive. Some had managed to crawl out of the windows, white and bruised, their nerves too shattered to allow them to be of much use to the injured. By the time Dr. Parkes and Mr. Fleming arrived upon the scene, the breakdown gang was on the spot, and their arrangements for rescuing the wounded were being energetically carried out. Unfortunately, being an excursion train, it was crowded with pleasure-seekers—the happy, light-hearted holiday-makers, little anticipating such a disastrous end to their day's outing; but fortunately no one was killed, though many were seriously wounded. Our interest lies chiefly with one. Dr. Parkes plunged into his work at once, and was busily engaged attending to those sufferers who had been already rescued and lifted on to the side of the track. Mr. Fleming, too, busied himself to the best of his ability, lending a hand, anywhere or in any way, where it was most needed.

"This way somebody, for God's sake!" exclaimed a voice at his elbow. Glancing up with a startled look, his eyes fell on Jack Swayne, with a white, scared look upon his face. Neither uttered a word of recognition or of surprise at this unexpected meeting. In moments of supreme excitement we do not express surprise at anything; indeed in the shaken state of our senses we don't even feel it.

" *He's here*," added Jack, in a horrified whisper; "he's hurt—he may be dead." He hurried Mr. Fleming along with him to where a knot of people were gathered at one spot, engaged in the endeavour to extricate some one who was buried beneath the *débris*. It was an elderly man, with iron-gray hair clinging matted and blood-stained about his temples; his hands lay nerveless; his eyes were closed, and his face looked as though it had been drained of every drop of blood. They had just succeeded in freeing him from his perilous position, and the rough bearded men, with hands gentle as the hands of women, lifted him on to the bank.

Dr. Parkes was speedily upon the spot, and he examined the injured man as well

as he was able to do under the circumstances. His professional eye evidently
regarded the case gravely, and having done
all he could do for the moment, he suggested
that the patient should be carried to the
nearest house. Perhaps some of the peas-
antry could be found willing to take care
of him; or perhaps he could be received and
better cared for at the Red Lion, the most
decent inn in the neighbourhood. Mr.
Fleming, who had been regarding the injured man with an inscrutable countenance,
and a hard cold glitter in his eyes, touched
the Doctor's arm lightly and inquired—

" Is he dangerously hurt ? "

" Somewhat seriously, I fear," he answered; "but I hope not dangerously. When
I can make a more thorough examination
I shall be able to give a more decided
opinion. Meanwhile, I know he will require good nursing and great care."

· " Which he cannot expect to get at the Red Lion," said Mr. Fleming ; " and at the cottage they certainly have no accommodation for an invalid. Let him be taken up to the Manor House; he will be sure of proper attention there."

" That is just the good, kind thing I should have expected of you ! " exclaimed Dr. Parkes, in hearty appreciation, as he turned to give orders for the removal without delay.

, " Can I take him in the carriage ? " inquired Mr. Fleming.

" You might," returned the Doctor, " but it would be difficult ; it is easier to improvise a litter. I'll see to that."

" And perhaps I had better hurry home to prepare the household for—what they are going to receive," he added slowly, unconsciously uttering the grace before meat.

" That will be best ; I'll see he is properly

despatched, and I'll follow myself as soon
as I have done all I can do here. Put him
to bed—his head and shoulders raised, and
bathe the wounds, but do nothing more till
I come."

Several other medical men had now
arrived upon the spot, and they helped in
lightening his labours. Jack, who had
heard his uncle's offer with amazement,
now stepped to his side, and whispered in
his ear—

"What are you thinking of? Is it well,
is it wise, to have *him* at the Manor
House?"

"Yes," replied Mr. Fleming, in the same
undertone. "It is best to have mine
enemy under mine own roof—there I can
keep good watch and ward over him. 'The
mad dog is best in his own kennel.'"

Jack seemed to understand his uncle's
motive, and acquiesced in his proposition.

The old man went with lagging steps, as
though his feet, as well as his heart, were
leaden weighted, towards his carriage.

" You are coming, my boy ? "

" Not while I can be of any use here,"
Jack answered ; then, as though struck by
a sudden thought, he added excitedly, before he turned away—

" Clarice ! in God's name, how can we
prepare her for this ? "

" I don't know—I'm dazed at present,"
he answered, passing his hand wearily across
his brow ; adding, " *She* must be our first
thought ; but she shall be cared for, Jack,
she shall be cared for—no fear of that."

Love seemed to give strength and decision
to his voice and to his spirit, for he stepped
briskly into the carriage and ordered the
coachman to call at Dr. Parkes's house on
the way home, and to " drive quickly."
The horses flew, as with winged feet, over

the ground, and in an incredibly short time stopped at the Doctor's residence. Miss Parkes and Clarice were strolling about the garden, waiting somewhat impatiently to learn what had really happened at the station. Mr. Fleming descended, with no signs of trepidation in his manner.

"I hope it was not a bad accident, father dear?" said Clarice, anxiously.

"Well, yes, my dear child, it has been a very serious accident, but it might have been worse."

"Everything that happens might be worse," exclaimed Miss Parkes, frigidly; "it is bad enough to be hanged, but it would be worse to be drawn and quartered."

Mr. Fleming humbly acquiesced, and then gave her her brother's message.

"I was to tell you not to expect him home till you see him. And Clarice, my dear, I have arranged for one of the injured

passengers to be taken up to the Manor
House—and—Miss Parkes, your brother was
good enough to suggest that this troublesome child of mine should remain with you
for a few days."

"But, father dear!" exclaimed Clarice,
"why cannot I come home and help in the
nursing?"

"You are better away," he answered;
"the gentleman is seriously injured. We
shall have our hands full—we don't know
how things may turn out. You know, dear
child, how nervous and sensitive you are!
It will lessen my anxieties to feel you are
well cared for here."

"You never sent me away before," said
Clarice, looking wistfully, half-suspiciously,
in his face. "When Jack was ill, I used to
read to him and help to amuse him."

"Jack was Jack, my dear," replied the
old man, smiling, "but this is—a stranger."

Seeing she was about to speak—perhaps fearing she would persist in returning home, and it was so hard, so unusual to refuse her anything, he added quickly, " I will see you again presently, but I must hurry away now; they are bringing him up, and if they arrive before me Hans may bar the gate—naturally they would not admit a wounded man into the house without my authority."

"But we only came out for a drive!" said the bewildered Clarice; " and I cannot stay without my clothes and things. I've got nothing to wear, and I must have——"

"True, true, my dear; I had forgotten. Well, I'll send Katrina down ; she'll bring all you want and settle you comfortably. But I really must go now—not a word, not another word ; I'll be back as soon as I have arranged matters at home." He turned to shake hands with Miss Parkes, adding, " I am sure you will excuse this sudden attack

on your hospitality—it is with your brother's
sanction; and on these occasions, etc., etc."

Miss Parkes expressed great pleasure at
receiving Clarice as her guest, and Mr.
Fleming having kissed her (Clarice, not
Miss Parkes) hurried away to the carriage,
and in another moment the horses were on
their homeward road as fast as they could
gallop.

"I'm not surprised that you don't care to
stay with us old folk, my dear," said Miss
Parkes, reproachfully. "I dare say it will
be rather dull for you; but the time has
been——"

"Oh, it isn't that!" exclaimed Clarice,
interrupting, with eyes fast filling with
tears. "Indeed I shall be as happy here as
anywhere, and it is very kind of you to have
me; but," she added with some emotion, "I
don't like to feel that—they don't want me
at home."

"Well, candidly, my dear, I agree with your papa; it is best that a delicate young creature like you should be out of the way of mortal miseries. I've seen a little of these things myself—the house full of groans and moans, legs or arms being cut off, and all sorts of horrors going on everywhere, enough to break nerves of steel : and you, my dear, who turn faint only at the sight of a cut finger! Depend upon it, you are best here—my brother thinks so, and he is always right."

Clarice was forced to rest content, though by no means pleased or satisfied with the arrangement. Meanwhile, on reaching home, Mr. Fleming called the household together; they were all old servants, who regarded themselves somewhat in the old fashion as part of the family, who served for love as well as for wages. Having explained that there had been a serious accident to the train, he

went on to inform them that in that very
train "Monsieur Lemaire was a passenger
to Penally. I am afraid he is somewhat
seriously hurt, and I have desired him to
be brought *here*, where he can be properly
attended to. I do not wish Miss Clarice
to know who is our inmate, *neither now
nor ever*. I need not say I rely on your
discretion and fidelity in all matters concerning your young mistress and myself; do
your duty as faithfully to this—gentleman,
as though you loved him, but answer no
questions, and give no information, concerning *us*." All listened respectfully while he
was speaking, and promised faithful obedience to his wishes. They were too well
trained to let the surprise they felt be
visible upon their countenances but when
they retired to their own domains their
wonderings broke loose, and their tongues
wagged fast and furiously; only Katrina,.

Clarice's faithful old nurse, remained behind, and looked inquiringly in Mr. Fleming's face, saying—

" What is going to happen, sir ? Why has he come ? Does he bring the *law* in his hand ? " Her voice quivered with emotion as she made these terse inquiries.

" I don't know why he has come, Katrina," answered Mr. Fleming, too deeply agitated to give any outward expression to his feelings ; " but it is for no good purpose, we may be sure ! But God knows best. At present he is not able to speak for himself."

" My *liebchen!* my poor innocent *liebchen!* " exclaimed her old nurse in the tenderest accents ; " but whatever happens, you will not let him take her away ? "

" I ! " exclaimed Mr. Fleming in bitter tones ; and a look of stern determination kindled in his eyes. " No. A promise to

the dead is sacred ; and at any risk, at any
cost, law or no law, I shall keep my word.
Now go ; they will be here- directly.   I
think you had better put him in the large
room next to Mr. Jack's dressing-room.
One of us should be always on the spot, or
at least within hearing."

While the household was busily preparing
for the reception of the unwelcome guest,
Mr. Fleming paced up and down the terrace,
harassed by many thoughts, watching and
waiting for the advent of his enemy.
Presently the little cavalcade came in sight.
A litter had been improvised at the station,
as easy as such a thing could be, and he was
carried all the way by men who had kindly
volunteered the service, they being relieved
in turn by other willing hands.   A small
knot of villagers gathered by the way and
trailed after them from the station, whispering and wondering among themselves " who

was this stranger? and why was he being taken to the Manor House?"

Let a catastrophe occur in even the most secluded part of the country, and it is astonishing how quickly a crowd of human beings gather round it. One wonders where they come from, for it often happens that not a human habitation is in sight—they seem to spring from anywhere, or nowhere; all crowd round, eager to have their share of the gruesome feast fate has provided for them. In the present instance there was nothing to see, nothing to be expected; an occasional groan from the injured man, and the sight of a white blood-stained face, as now and again, in restless unconscious pain, he tossed the covering off him—this was all the satisfaction they received after tramping the long distance under a burning sun. They only knew that some living, suffering fellow-creature was lying beneath that coarse covering, and that was enough to rouse that morbid curiosity which is common to all classes of society. The litter was carried into the Manor House and the doors closed behind it ; the crowd dissolved and went each their several ways, full of vague wondering.

Katrina installed herself as chief nurse in the sick-room. It was many years since they had met, and even when the wounded man regained consciousness she did not believe he would recognize her now, especially in the obscurity of the sick-room. They were hardly settled when Dr. Parkes arrived, and completed the brief examination which he had made upon the spot at the moment of the accident. Upon this more thorough examination, he decided that the injuries were not so serious as he had at first apprehended. Considering the nature of the accident, and the manner of his entanglement among the wrecked carriages, his escape was marvellous. Of course he was suffering from contused wounds, nervous prostration, and injuries to the head, which might render him unconscious for some time—perhaps only for a few hours, perhaps for a few days; he could not tell, but he hoped there would be no grave results.

Katrina, in her attentions to him, strictly obeyed the Doctor's instructions, and watched over him, indeed, with care and devotion as though she loved him. Throughout the household, every one stood, metaphorically speaking, on the tip-toe of wonderment. " Would he live ? would he die ? In either case what would happen ? " They went about the house, and carried on their daily business with noiseless footsteps, as though a dead man lay in the house; and in the evening when they gathered together in the servants'-hall, instead of settling down to amuse themselves in their usual fashion, they indulged in a game of speculation, and invented a new sum in arithmetic, where the balance was not carried forward in favour of their enforced guest.

CHAPTER XIII.

MRS. SPENCER DOES HER DUTY.

THE first moment that Mr. Fleming and Jack could have a quiet word together, they plunged at once into the subject of M. Lemaire.

"I am bewildered, and in the dark on all sides," exclaimed Mr. Fleming; "I know nothing but what your brief telegram told me, and the subsequent event which has thrown him upon my hands."

"And, indeed, my dear Uncle, there is little more to tell," replied Jack. "By merest, luckiest chance I met him in the Strand. I knew him at a glance——"

"And did he recognize you?" inquired Mr. Fleming, eagerly.

"How could he?" answered Jack; "he hasn't seen me for ten years, and from eighteen to twenty-eight a man changes considerably—besides I have grown a beard since then. No, he could not possibly know me. I followed him to his hotel—in a by-street leading out of the Strand; saw him housed, heard him order his dinner, and resolved to keep an eye upon him, for I suspected he was hatching some devil's mischief. Then I rushed off in search of a detective; I knew where to look for my man, and I found him—a capital fellow he is too. I told him briefly and exactly what I wanted; he warmed to his work beautifully. How he managed to get so quickly on terms with Lemaire, I don't know; but they spent that very evening *together*, dined and wined one another, and got quite sociable and confidential; and my friend Wagstaff found out all I wanted to know. Lemaire told a good story. 'He had come,' he said, 'all the way from South Africa to regain possession of his daughter, his only child, who had been surreptitiously withdrawn from his custody, and carried away and concealed in a remote corner of the country by mercenary relations. He is anxious about her welfare, he even fears for her life—as in the event of her death, the objectionable relatives would succeed to the immense property which she would inherit if she lived to become of age.'"

"The villain!" muttered Mr. Fleming from between his clenched teeth.

"Of course Wagstaff duly sympathized," continued Jack, "and wormed a few more interesting lies out of him, finishing up with the one important fact that, after wandering the world over, he had only just succeeded in discovering her whereabouts, and contemplated an immediate visit to Cornwall, intending to start this morning. Having ascertained the time of his departure, I was on the platform when he arrived. I took a ticket by the same train, got into the hindmost carriage, and—here we are. By a mere stroke of good luck, I have escaped from this accident scot-free; and he—Well, what is to be the next move?"

"Things are at rest now," replied Mr. Fleming; "there can be no move on either side till he recovers or—dies."

"Oh, he'll recover fast enough!" exclaimed Jack. "Men whose lives are of no use to anybody but their owners, never die. But how about Clarice—she is the chief object of our anxiety; does she know?"

"She knows nothing," was the answer; "and if it be possible to keep the matter from her, I don't intend her to know anything."

" How can you manage that?—how prevent their meeting, living here under the
same roof? "

" Ay, but they don't happen to be under
the same roof! " replied Mr. Fleming, with
a satisfied smile at his clever idea of keeping her away. " I have left her under Miss
Parkes's care, and hope to keep her there
till things are settled—under the excuse of
her delicacy and nervousness. Meanwhile,
I am resolved that, law or no law, under
no possible circumstances will I ever part
with Clarice, to give her into that man's
keeping. I think it would be expedient to
take Dr. Parkes into our confidence; we
must rely upon his prudence and discretion.
Of course he must suspect something from
our unusual course of action—and half-con-
fidences are as dangerous as no confidence
at all. If we try to keep him in the dark
he may get the wrong light thrown upon

the subject. He is already deeply interested
in Clarice, and when he is cognisant of the
truth, will give us, I am sure, his cordial
sympathy and co-operation."

Jack quite agreed as to the wisdom of the
proposed course. Accordingly, on his visit
the next morning Dr. Parkes was closeted
with Mr. Fleming in the privacy of his
study, where they were secure from interruption. Judging from the cordiality with
which they shook hands and parted, after
an hour's interview, there was no doubt but
that the one had secured the sympathy and,
so far as it was required, the co-operation of
the other.

It is needless to say that Clarice remained
an inmate of Dr. Parkes's residence for the
next ten days ; her favourite books, her
music, and a few trifling household gods
had been transferred thither, in order that
she might be as far as possible surrounded

by the atmosphere of home. Occasionally
she was exercised in mind as to her enforced
and prolonged absence from home, and was
inclined to rebel against it ; but Mr. Fleming
came to see her every morning, and gave her
some good reason for prolonging her stay
from day to day. Once, to her amazement,
in his uncle's stead came Jack ! Why had
he returned so unexpectedly to Cornwall?
He easily accounted for his visit. " He
had," he said, " a little business in hand, in
which his uncle was concerned ; and he
thought it best to run down himself and
talk the matter over, rather than let the
lawyers carry on an expensive correspondence, which might end in a muddle.
More business may be done in an hour's
interview than by a written ream of fools-
cap, and he had no idea of carrying on the
game of question, answer, and observation
for the lawyers' benefit; and since there

was trouble in the house—well, he thought
he would stay till it was over." So far, all
that he said was true, though it was not
politic to tell her all the truth. There
were always some legal points at issue on
which it was necessary that Mr. Fleming
should be consulted; certainly they might
be postponed for a season, but in order not
to outrage his conscience he took the
present opportunity of discussing them
with his uncle, so salving his conscience
and saving the lawyers' fees.

Perhaps the fact of his presence at the
Manor House did more towards reconciling
Clarice to remain away than all Mr.
Fleming's representations. Miriam Spencer
and Clarice spent very much of their time
together during these days; some subtle
chord of sympathy seemed to have grown
between them. They passed long mornings
reading, chatting, or working, and some-

times Jack took the girls for a drive, or
escorted them on a walking expedition—
dividing his attentions so equally that it
was difficult to tell to which he was really
most devoted; if anything, he was a shade
more tender to Miriam, and on every look,
tone, or gesture of his, she put her own con-
struction.

Her heart was gladdened thereby, and
filled with a hundred hopes and longings,
more sweet from the very uncertainty of
the fulfilment thereof. The life she had
hitherto lived, unloving and unloved,
seemed a vague, empty space—now it had
a far-stretching background of a thousand
sweet unsubstantial dreams. *He* who had
flooded the greyness of her life with love's
first sunshine had come back; and though
his lips told no "flattering tale," surely his
eyes were eloquent enough to do without
the use of speech! His voice—how sweet

and tender it seemed when he spoke to her! Surely he would speak one day !

So, possessed by the pure passion—which, let the world say what it will, is the one great good of life—the girl dreamed on. The dull, expressionless eyes softened and brightened with a new light; the harsh angles of the nature she had inherited from her parents were smoothed and rounded, and her character altogether underwent a subtle change. She grew more sympathetic and gentle; instead of the caustic sneer she dropped a kindly word, and while under the old influence she was hard and cold, under the new she tried to palliate the sin, and even cast about to find some excuse for the sinner. The ice of stultified Christianity melted 'from her frost-bound youth, and it grew rich in the bloom of faith, hope, and charity—the flowers of the true Christian's creed.

The Rectory folk felt the change, and were mightily puzzled thereat—the moral atmosphere of their home was somehow changed. They only lived for the bitter pleasure of harrying out, gloating over, and punishing the sins of other people; now their own child had ungratefully passed over to the other side, and not only brought forward " extenuating circumstances " against the verdict of " guilty," but, instead of pelting the sinner with pitiless frowns and phrases, positively talked of " toleration " and " kindness " being part of a Christian's duty! Oh, there was evidently something wrong—softening of the brain, or some mental twist that could be cured like a bodily fracture : they almost doubted whether Dr. Parkes ought not to be called in and consulted upon the matter. Meanwhile, as her appetite was normal, her sleeping and walking powers good, they

waited some further development before
they incurred a doctor's bill.

Meanwhile Miriam was not allowed to
take sole possession of Clarice. Mrs.
Spencer came to the fore—she feared "lest
the dear girl should be dull away from
home;" besides she saw an opportunity of
doing some good. She had not much opinion
of the Christianity of the Manor House,
though they certainly did come to church
once every Sunday: yet Clarice did not pay
proper attention; she looked preoccupied
and dreamy except when she was singing—
she seemed to enjoy that, and to put more
earthly enjoyment than was proper into the
religious exercise. As for Mr. Fleming, he
was constantly known to go fast asleep
during the sermon; and though the Rector
thumped the cushions, and tried by fierce
denunciations and threats of eternal punishment to awaken the slumbering sinner, he

still slept on, and when the service was over walked serenely out of church, smiling and content like a man who feels he has done his duty. Of course all that was very wrong, but she could not take him by the ears and scold him, as she did her poorer parishoners if they dared even to blink.

However, here was an opportunity of putting Clarice through the parish business, and letting her see the amount of work and iniquity the Church had to contend against. Clothed in the armour of righteousness, she went forth to fight the Philistines, searching for some skeleton which she was sure was hidden in some corner of every house in the village. She was eager to enlighten Clarice's mind by the sight of the conflict. But the sight of sin, poverty, and sorrow, was not new to Clarice; she and Mr. Fleming had familiarized themselves with the poor of Penally, and many humble homes were brighter and happier for their unostentatious visits. They gave freely and judiciously where there was need; they helped the poor to help themselves, and neither oppressed with charity nor wearied with expostulations. They had a kind encouraging word even for the hardened sinner, so feeding the starved soul as well as the hungry body. Where is the use of preaching virtue where people are wanting bread?

They had already established pleasant relations with the poor of the parish; a chord of sympathy ran like a current of electricity from the Manor House to the poorest house in Penally, connecting the rich and poor by the bond of common humanity. The " Manor House gentry," and the " Rectory folk," were as opposite in the eyes of the villagers as are the heavens and earth. The first was always

welcome, the latter avoided. They hated
to see Mrs. Spencer's beady eyes and sharp
nose poking in at their cottage doors; she
was too good at giving gratuitous advice,
too eager in her fight against their domestic
arrangements; no fancied unsanitary state
of things was allowed to flourish within her
ken; she hunted down *imaginary* fever dens,
and superintended the cleansing and fumi-
gating process herself, caught little ragged
runagates and packed them off to school.
When she came near there was a general
scrimmage among the urchins, and a stam-
pede of the skulking idlers who dared to
lounge in their doorways.

Poor Mrs. Spencer! she meant well, but
she took hold of things at the wrong end;
her faults were venal, her virtues relentless.
People of her peculiar character are perhaps
more to be pitied than blamed; they have
no real, confidential friends, no sympathies;

they are as much shut out of the inner life
of their " dearest friends " as the dead lying
in their graves are shut out of the sunlight !
For who could expose a bruised heart or
wounded spirit to cold cynicism or bitter
probe of a woman's caustic tongue ? We
all have some dear friend to whom we can
confide our servants' delinquencies, our mil-
linery troubles, or the open scandals of the
kettledrum ; but from our hearts and from
our inner selves they are rigorously excluded.

One bright morning Mrs. Spencer took
Clarice and Miriam on her inquisitorial
campaign. She swept like an angry whirl-
wind into one house, and out of another,
castigating everybody with her tongue, and
when she could not scold, maintained a grim
dissatisfied silence. She was surprised to
see Clarice welcomed with smiles, and by
no means so great a stranger as she had
supposed ; little children ran out and clung

shyly to her skirts, unrebuked for dirty hands and unkempt heads; grey-haired, hard-working folks welcomed her as a bit of sunshine into their squalid homes; and the sullen faces of the few lazy loungers, who were the pests of the village, cleared up, and, instead of skulking and hiding like lost, crushed creatures, they came out from their wretched hovels, to intercept a smile or catch a word from her lips. Somehow, the greater the wrong-doer, the more misguided the human soul, the more pitiful she felt towards them; and if only her silent shadow fell across their path, it gave them at least a desire, if not an impetus, to scramble out of the slough of despond, and once more tread in the straight and better way. She knew them all by name, and could ask after this old woman's rheumatism, or that old man's gout—all of which was very distasteful to Mrs. Spencer, as evidence of a vulgar mind; but of course she could say nothing about it, and only kept a discreet, condemnatory silence.

"Dear Mrs. Spencer, please stop one minute!" exclaimed Clarice, as they came to a narrow muddy lane, with some tumble-down cottages scattered on either side; "I must drop in to look after one of my pensioners—I've not been near her for a week."

Mrs. Spencer strode after her, saying—

"My dear, you should really take advice before you rush into these sort of places—only the most disreputable people live hereabouts."

"They are just the kind of people that require most looking after," rejoined Clarice; "'they that are whole need not a physician,' you know, 'but those that are sick.'"

"Don't quote Scripture in that loose fashion, my dear," exclaimed Mrs. Spencer; "it is irreverent, if not blasphemous."

Without noticing the rebuke, Clarice glanced forward.

"Why, there is my old friend Kitty Penrith, sitting in the doorway enjoying the sunshine!" she exclaimed; "I'm glad to see her able to get about."

Mrs. Spencer caught her arm, and forced her to turn round and stand still.

"My poor, motherless child," she said, compassionately, "it is my duty to speak to you. I dare not be silent, or you will be lost in this sea of infamy!"

"What do you mean?" inquired the astonished Clarice.

"That old woman, Kitty Penrith," she answered, "is the greatest impostor and worst woman in the neighbourhood."

"Impossible!" exclaimed Clarice; "she is helpless, she suffers so much she is almost bedridden! There must be some mistake surely *she* can do no harm!"

" She does all the harm she can. A worm can't crawl as fast as a horse can gallop, and a cat can't do as much harm as a wild beast ; but if a crippled sinner sins all she can, she's as bad as the biggest sinner alive ! "

" Mrs. Spencer, you frighten me with this mysterious way of talking," said Clarice. " Whatever the poor creature has done, I am sure she is sorry for it now."

" Not at all," she answered ; " besides, we never can repent as fast as we can sin. She glories in the most barefaced encouragement of vice, and when I talked to her, and tried to bring her to a sense of decency, she said I was no Christian, and ordered me —*me*, the Rector's wife !—out of her hovel, and threatened me with her crutch ! There!" she added, triumphantly ; " now you see the sort of thing you're going in for ! "

" But you don't tell me what dreadful thing she has done! " exclaimed Clarice.

"Humph! it is not pleasant to talk about it; but if you won't take my word, if you will discuss this very unsavory subject——" With a slight shrug of her shoulders, she added, "Since you know Kitty Penrith so well, I suppose you know her daughter Jane?"

"Oh yes, of course I do—poor Jane! A pale, sad-looking girl, with a pretty, curly-headed little boy."

"Ay! there's the trouble," rejoined Mrs. Spencer, quickly. "Jane was a fine-looking rosy girl when she went to service at Penzance, and doing well, so everybody thought. When one bitter winter day she came back unexpectedly, sick and bedraggled, bad in health and bad in morals, and Kitty Penrith, in the most barefaced way, had the child born in the house!"

"But surely there was no harm in that?" observed Clarice.

"You're too innocent—you don't understand," explained Mrs. Spencer. "That
child had no business in the world at all;
it ought never to have been born, my dear,
and that's the fact; and instead of being
ashamed of it, they are as fond and proud of
the brat, and dress it and curl its hair, as
though it was somebody's child, and had a
right to be here—and the old woman is the
worst of the two!"

"But surely you can't blame the mother
for having pity on her unfortunate child?"

"People have no business to be unfortunate," answered Mrs. Spencer, with a
snap as though she had caught the sinner
between her teeth and crushed it.

"How can we expect God to have com-
passion upon us, if we have so little mercy
on one another?" said Clarice, half speaking to herself.

"We don't expect it, my dear," replied

Mrs. Spencer, brusquely ; "we are told plainly enough that the portion of the wicked is hell-fire, where there ' shall be weeping and gnashing of teeth.' But about these people, my dear : after what I have told you, I hope there will be an end to your pernicious charity."

" Quite the contrary ! " exclaimed Clarice, decidedly ; " I am more interested now than I was before. I shall speak to my father about them, and I am sure he will find some way of improving and changing their condition."

" They were nearly changing that them-selves a few months ago," rejoined Mrs. Spencer, " for the villain who is responsible for that child's unlicensed existence was actually coming home from the Cape to marry her ! "

" And why didn't he ? " asked Clarice, eagerly.

"Because he couldn't—he was drowned on his way home; and the hussy had the impudence to tie on some black rags—as though she had a right to go into mourning —and come to church, and was actually heard sobbing over her prayers! I think there ought to be a law against such irreverent exhibitions in a place of worship."

"Come unto me all ye that are weary and heavy laden, and I will give you rest," were the words that floated through Clarice's mind; but she said nothing. She felt it was hardly seemly to enter a protest against the Rector's wife—a woman, too, so much older than herself. But Miriam exclaimed, in a pained voice—

"But, mother, she was so unhappy. I was always sorry for that poor girl; perhaps she loved him!"

"That is a most indecent expression, and I should never have expected a child of mine to utter it!" said Mrs. Spencer, severely. "As a rule, people who are so fond of excusing immoralities are far on the way towards committing them; but you are very much changed for the worse, lately— you seem to be under some bad influence!"

Bouncer, who, as usual, was in attendance on his young mistress, had rushed forward as though he was quite familiar with the way, and disappeared into Kitty's cottage, scaring her cat and a couple of ragged fowls by the way. He was heard barking joyously, and in another moment emerged from it, with a bright-eyed, yellow-haired boy cling- ing to his neck, and making futile attempts to mount upon his back; when a young woman rushed out, glared irefully down the road, and dragged him back into the house, administering a vigorous shaking by the way. Mrs. Spencer had turned, and was walking slowly back to the high-road.

"One minute, please, Mrs. Spencer," exclaimed Clarice, as she bounded forward,
disappeared for the space of a few seconds
into the cottage, and then, half-breathlessly,
hurried to rejoin her companions on the
highway.

"You are a dear, good girl!" exclaimed
Mrs. Spencer, with an air of patronizing
satisfaction, arguing well from Clarice's
quick return. "It is quite pleasant to
give advice when it has such a good
effect. I should like to speak a few warn-
ing words to your dear father; and I
would, too, if I thought he would take
it in good part—no offence taken or meant
on either side."

"My father is never offended at anything
that is kindly meant."

"Of course, I am naturally anxious for
the good of our parishioners—indeed I may
say I devote my life to their service; and it

is disheartening to find people who ought to know better pulling in an opposite direction, even with the best intentions."

"Yes?" exclaimed Clarice, interrogatively, waiting for further information.

"Poor, dear Mr. Fleming," continued Mrs. Spencer, "I am sure he is a thoroughly good man, and means well.— You must excuse me, my dear, but since we are speaking on this subject, it is best to speak plainly.—He wishes to do good, but he is altogether wrong-headed, like yourself; and instead of helping to abolish crime, he becomes an aider and abettor of it."

"I think you are mistaken," exclaimed Clarice, with heightened colour; "you do not understand either him or his ways."

"My dear child, it is all as plain as a pikestaff," answered Mrs. Spencer. "When a man of position stoops to the companion-ship of loose-livers and drunkards, he becomes to a great extent responsible for their vices."

"Who does this?" inquired Clarice, indignantly. "Surely you dare not bring such an accusation against my father!"

"Here is a simple case in point," continued Mrs. Spencer. "Ben—you know Ben, up at the station?—the miserable heathen doesn't even own to a surname—well, he lost his place through neglecting his duties, oversleeping himself in the sunshine, or something or another; and since then he has been loafing about, drinking and drinking, whenever he could get a chance. Well, the other day he was lying dead-drunk on the road, and Mr. Fleming, your father, was actually seen to help him up, take him by the arm, all covered with mud and dust as he was, and lead him towards his miserable home—not rating him as he deserved, but coaxing him along

in quite a friendly way ! I shouldn't wonder
if he put him to bed, and sent him some
soup afterwards ! Ugh ! it's dreadful; such
a bad example, too ! "

A soft smile played round Clarice's lips
as she said—

" Just like him, the dear old dad ! Surely,
Mrs. Spencer, you must acknowledge that
it is better to lead a man away from drink
with a kind hand, than drive him towards it
with hard words ? "

Mrs. Spencer smiled her usual super-
cilious self-satisfied smile, as though she
looked from a supreme height on all the
world below as she answered—

" My poor child, you take such an extra-
ordinary crooked view of everything, I am
afraid you will have to undergo a surgical
operation before you can see things rightly.
—Why do you look at me so strangely ? "
she added, sharply.

"I was only thinking," said Clarice, thoughtfully, " if ever you have to suffer—if any great tragic trouble overtakes you—how sorry I shall be ! "

CHAPTER XIV.

IT was about the third day after the accident. M. Lemaire had not regained a moment's consciousness, but lay as a rule quiet enough, only occasionally tossing on his pillow and moaning. For some hours, however, he had been—at least so Katrina thought—in a profound sleep; and when Dr. Parkes paid his usual visit, he smiled, and said " his patient was on the mend; " the breathing was less laboured and more natural; the skin, from being harsh and dry, was soft and moist, evidently regaining its natural colour.

" He is on the road to recovery," said the
Doctor; "he only needs quiet and care—let
him have perfect rest. When he first recovers consciousness, you must be especially
careful that he does not get excited on any
subject whatever."

Katrina, of course, promised obedience and
watchfulness. The Doctor having departed,
she busied herself about the room, settling
everything for the invalid's comfort, arranging the bed-curtains so as to exclude
as much as possible the light from him.
She opened the window to let in the warm,
soft air; sniffed and rubbed her nose, as it
was her habit to do in any perplexity; then
put on her spectacles, and busied herself
with some household sewing. Her wrinkled
face was full of expression, and her small
black eyes were as bright and eager as they
were twenty years ago. Occasionally, as
she glanced at the sick man with a lowering

brow, evidently with no goodwill towards
him, she muttered to herself in an irritable
sort of way. The faithful soul had plenty
to think about. She knew all the "ins
and outs" of the family mysteries, and their
troubles were her own.

Presently she heard the patient stir, and
noticed a difference in his breathing; on
looking round she saw that his eyes were
wide open, and fixed upon her face. She
went to the bedside and smoothed his
pillow, and arranged the bed-clothes as she
said—

"Glad to see you taking notice, sir—
you're better."

"Better!" he echoed, rather faintly;
"what has been the matter? Have I
been ill?" His voice sounded unused and
hollow, and he looked vaguely round the
room as though he had awakened in a new
world.

"Yes, indeed you have ; but you are improving now," she answered. "But you had best lie quiet ; you mustn't talk much, till the Doctor gives you leave to."

For a few moments he did lie still, with knit brows, as though he were trying to clear the mists from his brain and remember something. Presently he said—

"Who are you? I fancy I have heard your voice! Undraw the curtains and let me see your face."

"It would do you no good to see it," she answered, " and I am forbidden to let in the light ; " and she drew the curtains closer.

"It's very strange," he muttered, as his head rolled restlessly on his pillow ; "all so confused I can't remember anything. At least tell me where I am, and how I came here ; and—whose house is this?"

"My master's," she answered, " and that's quite enough for you to know at present."

"And who the devil is your master, woman?" he exclaimed with angry emphasis.

"Oh well, if you're going to swear, it's a symptom!" she answered coolly; "we shall have to put you into a straight-waistcoat. But I hear the doctor coming up the drive—you can ask him as many questions as you please."

In the course of a few minutes Dr. Parkes entered the room, and regarded his patient with the usual grave professional eye. He did not seem surprised to find that he had regained consciousness, and was alive to things passing round him; though so far as memory was concerned he was still groping in the dark, and was faint and weak from the excitement already stirring in his brain. He began to pour into the Doctor's ear a host of voluble half-incoherent questions; to which he vouchsafed no reply, but spoke to him soothingly as he would have spoken to a fractious child.

" See here, M. Lemaire," he said gravely, " you have been seriously ill, though you are recovering now, and if you wish the improvement to continue you must keep perfectly quiet awhile longer. I will see you again to-morrow, and if you are as much better as I hope you will be if you obey my instructions, I will answer any questions you may desire to ask. This is a critical time ; " he added, " you must keep your mind quiet and free from excitement, or you will undo all the good that has been done. There, don't talk any more. I can rely on your nurse's discretion. Sleep, sleep, all you can, and keep yourself from thinking. Ask no questions ; I have forbidden your being answered."

M. Lemaire had great recuperative powers, and by the next day had made such rapid strides towards recovery, that when Dr. Parkes arrived he found him sitting up in bed, rating and grumbling at Katrina, who obeyed the Doctor's instructions to the letter and gave him no information whatever, but only irritated him the more by insisting that he should keep quiet and hold his tongue.

"I am glad you have come, Doctor," he said, stretching out a long bony hand like a bird's claw; "I am stronger now. My thoughts are coming back: I am beginning to remember. With a little help, I shall soon be all right. Come, sit down," he added feverishly, as he passed his hand over his forehead, "and tell me everything that has happened; if you only give me a clue, I think my memory will wake up and follow it."

But the Doctor was not to be hurried in that way, nor led to plunge at once into the

troubled waters ; he went deliberately to
work—he felt the patient's pulse, and
made such other inquiries as were professional and necessary. But M. Lemaire
fretted and fumed under the examination,
and snatched his hand from the Doctor's ex-
claiming—

"There, there! I don't want any more
pulse-feeling nonsense ; all this silence and
mystery irritates and worries me, and keeps
my pulse beating like a steam-hammer. I
want to be satisfied, to have my mind set
at rest—to know where I am, and how I
came here. I see nobody but that—that
woman who——" (he indicated Katrina,
who occupied her usual seat by the window,
and with spectacled nose sat knitting).

"Has been your careful and most faithful
nurse," interrupted the Doctor.

"Yes, yes! I know she had been all that,"
he rejoined, testily, "but she makes my

flesh creep when she touches me. She never talks, but moves about noiseless as a shadow, like some weird, eerie thing; and when she smooths my pillow, and her hands pass over me, I feel as though she were streaking me for my grave. And it is not fancy, Doctor, but often in the night, while I was un-conscious—I felt with my brain rather than saw with my eyes—she brought people in, and they stood at my bedside, looked at me, sometimes touched me, and whispered to-gether, as though they were plotting some-thing horrible together; then they glided out of the room like ghosts. I could not move, I could not see or speak, but I felt and knew! What does it all mean?"

"It means, my dear sir, that your brain is weak, and in a state of morbid agitation and unnatural excitement," answered the Doctor.

"It will be in a state of agitation and

unrest till I am satisfied. You said you
would tell me everything. See how calm
I am now! I wait, I listen—tell me all that
has happened, so far as you know."

Dr. Parkes saw that it would be injurious
to keep M. Lemaire any longer in ignorance as to his whereabouts; the refusal to
give him the information he required would
do him more harm in his present state of
irritation than any knowledge of absolute
facts could possibly do; so he added, cautiously—

"The fact is, M. Lemaire, you have been
in a terrible accident, which, but for God's
mercy, might have been a fatal one."

"An accident! Yes!" with a look of eager
interrogation, knitting his brows as though
he was trying to recall some wandering
thoughts.

"A railway accident," continued the
Doctor, impressively; "the engine ran off

the line, the carriages toppled one over the other, and you were extricated from the wreck, hurt, unconscious, but mercifully alive. This railway ticket was found in your possession."

M. Lemaire sprang up in the bed, stretched out his hand and seized it eagerly. The Doctor kept a keen, scrutinizing look upon his face.

" Penally ! " he exclaimed, crushing the ticket in his hand as he fell back in the bed, and with closed eyes remained for a moment silent, muttering to himself. Then he partly raised himself up, adding aloud : " A light breaks upon me ! I remember now ! I did take the train for Penally. I remember nothing more distinctly—only a crash, a flash as though a hundred fires were lighted in my brain, and nothing more. Where did the train break down ? Where am I now ? "

He flung himself forward almost upon the Doctor's shoulder, and gripped him with his long bony fingers, and gazed eagerly on his face as though he would seize the answer before the tongue had power to utter it.

" The train was wrecked within a few hundred yards of Penally station," replied the Doctor, " and you were brought here, where you have been well cared for and nursed so far on the way to recovery."

" And where is *here ?* " inquired M. Lemaire, testily. " Whose house is this? and who is the master who does not deign to look in upon his guest ? "

" When you are willing to receive him I am sure he will not be slow in paying you a visit," returned Dr. Parkes.

" But who is this ' *he ?* '—his name ? "

" Is Fleming."

" My God ! in Philip Fleming's house !

helpless, in his power! and yet I live!" He sank back upon his pillow, as though that name had struck him senseless.

Dr. Parkes sat silent by the bedside, leaving things to take their natural course in his patient's mind; he, at least, had no power to direct or guide them—neither, indeed, did he know how it would be wise that they should be directed or guided— through the bewildering labyrinth through which they must be wandering. It is always difficult to legislate for other people; even when we know the difficulties of the situation, we can neither see nor comprehend the complex working of the mental machinery, the battle of the myriad thoughts and feelings which fight a hard fight in silence and darkness, making no stir, no ripple on the outer current of life. The actions born of the inward struggle are alone visible to the world's eyes, which can only judge of the fact, and knows nothing of the battle which has been lost or won. We can only judge of the open actions of our fellow men and women; the motive and chief mainspring of such actions is and must always be hidden from our sight.

Dr. Parkes waited for his patient to make the first sign; he would not by a single word disturb the current of his thoughts. After a long silence, during which his heavy breathing was alone heard, he turned his face—now cadaverous in its pallor, and bearing the marks of an inward struggle—and fixed his eyes upon the Doctor's face as he said in a low voice, almost a whisper, for he seemed quite exhausted—

"Doctor, was it chance that brought me here, or fate?"

"A most fortunate chance for you," began the Doctor, "that Mr. Fleming happened to be on the spot and recognized you.

You would not have fared so well with strangers."

"Oh, if they had only put me on a shutter, a hurdle, and taken me anywhere—anywhere but here!"

"And yet, pardon me, M. Lemaire, but I thought that I understood that you came here purposely to see Mr. Fleming?"

"But not to break bread under his roof; not to be helpless on his hands. Doctor, you must get me away! I am strong—you don't know how strong; but I cannot, I will not, stay another hour under this roof."

"Come, come, M. Lemaire," said the Doctor, soothingly, "if you agitate yourself in this way I will not answer for the consequences. You have nothing to fear from Mr. Fleming; he will not intrude upon you till you desire to receive him. Be reasonable and keep calm. Whatever business you may have to transact with Mr. Fleming can be discussed in a simple, straightforward fashion, as soon as you are strong enough to enter into such relations; at present you are really too weak to undergo any mental excitement."

" Weak in body—yes—but mentally I am strong and calm now. I know precisely what I want to say to Mr. Fleming, and am as well able to speak to him now as I was before this happened to me. Ah, Doctor! flesh and blood can't bear too much, and you do not know how many wrongs I have that must be righted ! He has stolen——"

" Hush ! " exclaimed the Doctor, laying his hand upon his patient's lips ; " do not discuss your family affairs with me. I am your physician only, not your confidant."

" Then, as a physician, you must know that the body cannot recover while the mind is so fiercely agitated as mine is. A quiet brain, and the power to face mine enemy fairly, is all that I require now, and that I shall never get here, under this roof. I *must* go ! I *must !* "

Before any one could prevent him he sprang from his bed, and began scrambling for his clothes. But "Man proposes, and God disposes." The exertion was too much for him ; he reeled and would have fallen, but Dr. Parkes caught him in his arms and laid him gently in his bed.

With slow returning consciousness, the forcible fact impressed itself on M. Lemaire's mind that the Doctor was right, and he was not fit for any mental or physical exer-tion yet; he must yield to the inevitable and bide his time. The spirit was willing, but the flesh was weak. From this interview with Dr. Parkes, when the fact of his where-abouts was first made known to him, he alluded no more to the subject; he neither fretted nor fumed, nor rebelled in the

slightest degree against the Doctor's will,
but obeyed his instructions with perfect
docility. So far the Doctor was himself surprised at the sudden change ; he could not
understand it. Had the fire of his excitement died out ? or was it only smouldering
to blaze out presently fiercer than before ?
As a physician, he was satisfied that his
patient was making such rapid strides, he
would soon be altogether off his hands. As
for M. Lemaire, we cannot follow the work-
ings of his mind as he lay silent, still, and
watchful in his bed, or sat, with his chair
wheeled to the window, looking out upon
the beautiful land- and sea-scape whereon
Clarice loved to look and dream and wonder.

During the earlier part of his illness, and
while he was still a stranger to her identity,
he had evinced a strange dislike, a shrinking
away from Katrina, even when she ad-
ministered most to his comfort. Now he

was changed utterly—his manner to her was all that could be desired, and he expressed the most grateful appreciation of her care and kindness. Only on one occasion did he allude to any former acquaintance. It happened in this wise. He had been out for the first time for a turn on the terrace, and he returned to his room apparently very much fatigued. He lay back in his chair quite quiet for a time ; his eyes were half closed in a kind of cat's sleep, but he was watching Katrina, who sat knitting opposite to him with her owl-eyed glasses on her nose ; and she was quite aware of the fact, and prepared for any kind of attack he might make upon her. Presently, in a soft, purring voice, he said—

" How strangely things repeat themselves in this world, Katrina ! How many years it is—and yet it seems no time ago—since I saw you sitting exactly as you are sitting

now, watching over another invalid as you
are now watching over *me.*"

" Ah! " ejaculated Katrina, shortly ; " *she*
died, unluckily ; *you*—live ! "

" Unluckily too, you think, though you
don't like to say it," he rejoined, with a low,
chuckling laugh, half smothered in his
throat. " Ah! Katrina, you are prejudiced.
You misjudge me, like the rest of the
world."

" That can't matter to you, sir. I am
only a servant," she answered.

" You were my poor wife's friend. Why
can't you be mine ? Why will you league
with my enemies against me ? "

" One can't serve God and the devil too,"
she answered.

" Sharp-tongued as ever," he remarked ;
" but I excuse your disloyalty to me in consideration of what you were to *her*, for after
all that has happened I have no ill-feeling
towards you," he added.

"None to spare for poor folk like me," she answered, plying her needles more vigorously than before, and closing her heart close as a steel-trap, determined he should wheedle nothing out of *her*. A few minutes' pause; then, stooping forward and laying his hand with an arresting motion upon her arm, he added, in his softest, most insinuating tones—

"It is no use beating about the bush. You know I have been away in Africa, and lost sight of everything and everybody for all these years. Can't you tell me something? I will make it worth your while. You must see that I want to know," he added impatiently, "about my daughter. Is she well? and *where* is she? I must, I will know something about my child!"

"Ask Mr. Fleming; you will see him to-morrow," Katrina answered, as she rose up and left the room.

His eyes followed her with a look of bitter hatred that needed not the emphasis of words. He shook his fist menacingly as the door closed upon her, and with a muttered curse upon his lips glared out across the scented wilderness, and caught a glimpse of Mr. Fleming and Jack Swayne, who were walking slowly up and down in the shadow of the wood, evidently deeply interested in the subject they were discussing.

CHAPTER XV.

M. LEMAIRE was up and dressed long before the clock struck twelve—the hour arranged for the interview between him and Mr. Fleming. He was alone— no Katrina sat knitting in the window, where she had sat for so many days. Her attentions being no longer needed, she had vacated her place. He paced impatiently up and down the room, with bent brows and compressed lips, arranging his thoughts and his course of action, as though life were a chess-board, and he could play his own game thereon.

The window was wide open; the birds were singing, and the fresh sea-breeze, laden with the sweet fragrance from the flower garden, swept freely into the room. Everything without was still and peaceful; it seemed as though the very calm on the serene face of nature clashed with and fretted his restless spirit. Now and then he paused and looked out upon the sunlit scene; but his eye saw nothing, cared nothing for its beauty. The world is a very beautiful world when there are no discords in our own hearts, no jangling chords in our own nature, which set us at odds with ourselves and all the world beside.

Punctuality was a virtue cultivated at the Manor House, and as the clock struck twelve there was a rap at the door, and Hans appeared with the inquiry, " Was M. Lemaire at liberty to receive his master now ? "

"I am ready and waiting," was the answer, uttered with a scowling brow and an imperious tone. In another moment, Mr. Fleming, looking perhaps a shade paler than usual, entered the room. M. Lemaire stood with his hand resting on the back of a chair. Both men inclined their heads slightly, and then stood face to face, each looking in the other's eyes as though to measure his strength, and then waited for the first move in the wordy war that was to come. Mr. Fleming was the first to speak. Motioning M. Lemaire to sit down, he placed himself opposite to him, and said in cool, though perfectly polite tones—

"I am glad you are better, M. Lemaire. If I have not personally inquired after you before, it was from motives of delicacy that I refrained from doing so."

"Your motives of delicacy! Ah! I never questioned them; but somehow I have

always failed to appreciate them," replied
M. Lemaire, in sneering accents. "I suppose I ought to thank you for the attention
I have received under your roof. Well,
consider I have done so—though, if I had
been consulted, I would rather have been
left to rot on the roadside than owe my life
to you. An enforced debt is grudgingly
paid."

Mr. Fleming bowed his head graciously
as he answered—

"Unfortunately, you were not in a position to be consulted, or you might have had
your will. We need allude no further to
the subject. The *then* is past; the question
is the *now.* I presume your visit to Penally
was in search of *me.* Your business? Tell
me as briefly as you can."

"Does that need any explanation?" said
M. Lemaire.

"I think so," said Mr. Fleming, briefly,

as if determined to watch his words and waste no more than was necessary.

"A father seeking his child would need no explanation in the world's eyes," said M. Lemaire, with the most hypocritical calm.

"Father!" echoed Mr. Fleming, with bitter emphasis. "How dare you misuse the word? In what single instance have you ever done a father's duty? How dare you lay claim to the daughter you have never seen—whom you have neglected and deserted from her birth?"

"It was the force of circumstances," began M. Lemaire.

"The force of the devil, sir!" exclaimed Mr. Fleming, angrily, "who cuts out and fills up the lives of such men as you!"

"I have not come here to listen to your abuse, and I don't care for your criticism on my conduct. I only want my daughter Clarice. I have found you now, and I will hang on to your track like a bloodhound till I gain possession of my child. Where is she ? "

" Where you will never find her! " said Mr. Fleming, gravely.

" Not dead—not dead ? " exclaimed M. Lemaire, and such a flame of joy flashed from his eyes. Mr. Fleming could have stretched out his hand and strangled him on the spot; but he resolved to hold his self-possession fast, so he only answered—

" No, not dead, thank God."

" I thank God too! " exclaimed M. Lemaire; but an eager, crafty look replaced the triumphant fire as it faded from his eyes.

" You lie! " replied Mr. Fleming, coolly but emphatically. " You know her death would be the sweet news you have waited for—how long? "

" You would never gain a prize at mind-reading; you fly too wide of the mark," re-

joined M. Lemaire. "But I cannot be held
accountable for your evil thoughts. The
right is on my side, and I have nothing
more to do, except to relieve you of all
responsibility so far as my dear child is concerned. So far you have charged yourself
with her custody. . I shall now trouble you
to give her into *mine*. *I* am her natural
guardian."

. "My God, Lemaire! what a villain you
are!" exclaimed Mr. Fleming. "Is it worth
your while to wear a mask with me, who
know you so well? I can follow every
move you make. I know the aim and object of your coming *now*."

"I may perhaps add. one item to your
occult knowledge," rejoined M. Lemaire,
watching his countenance as though he
knew he was going to inflict upon him an
open wound. "I am going back to South
Africa, and naturally desire to make my

daughter's acquaintance and secure her companionship. I have neglected her too long, and am now anxious to make up for lost time."

" I am sorry to deprive you of the antici-pated pleasure ; but I am afraid you must go to South Africa alone. It is impossible that Clarice can accompany you," said Mr. Fleming, calmly, but firmly.

The two men looked at each other curi-ously. Each knew the other's hand and mode of playing perfectly well; at the same time each believed that he held the highest trump-card to win in the end. They ad-vanced cautiously, feeling their way, as it were, inch by inch.

" Why impossible ? " urged M. Lemaire. " The matter lies in your hands. You have only to bring us together, and I will answer for the result."

Mr. Fleming compressed his lips as

though to keep back the words he longed to utter; but answered nothing. Irritated by his silence, M. Lemaire foolishly unmasked his battery, saying excitedly—

"You have no right to keep my daughter in concealment! It is an illegal act to hide her from her lawful guardian. Remember, Mr. Fleming, Clarice is nearly two years under age."

"I have not forgotten that;" adding, with peculiar significant emphasis which seemed to sting his opponent into a state of fury, "but under your care I fear she might not live to be of age at all!"

The look of terrible meaning which settled in the old man's eyes could not have been lost, except upon a blind man. It struck M. Lemaire like a blow, but he never quailed. He did not show how keenly he felt it. He received it like a feather on a shield of brass, and tossed it lightly from

him. He smiled with scornful bravado as
he said : " Your baseless insinuation goes for
nothing in point of fact or in point of law,
and if you determine to oppose my rightful
claim I shall appeal to the law."

" And *I* shall be willing to answer to the
law," said Mr. Fleming, impressively. " M.
Lemaire, I promised your dying wife that
rather than let her child fall into your hands
I would lay her in the grave beside her ;
and I think, if goaded to the bitter end, I
should have strength to keep my word."

" My wife ! He ! he ! " chuckled M. Lemaire, under his breath. " Which wife ?
what wife ? I thought you went shares in
that business, and we divided the honours
between us ! A pretty story—quite a nine
days' wonder, indeed, if it were told in a
police-court ! It would have an ugly look
for *you,* the aristocratic, high-bred gentleman ! How dare you treat me so ? " he

added, in a rougher, louder tone. "Why, it is owing to *my* mercy that she whom you called your wife was not arraigned at the criminal bar for bigamy!"

"You *dared* not do it!" replied Mr. Fleming, not in the slightest degree disturbed. "Was it for her sake, or for mine, you spared her? Was it not rather that you feared lest your own diabolical doings would rise to the surface and confound you? We sinned—if sin it was; God knows I cannot judge—with our eyes shut: you with your eyes wide open. Let me recapitulate the facts—the plain, unvarnished facts as they would stand in the world's eyes. I married your wife—true, I admit the fact freely; but why, and how did that marriage come about? Let us go back and pick up the threads a few years earlier. A foolish father left me guardian to his child, Clara Duncombe—does the name strike you?"

"I had almost forgotten it," rejoined M. Lemaire, shrugging his shoulders.

"I watched the pretty, playful child develope into a beautiful girlhood, sweet and pure as the sun-dew; and, although I was then in the sere and yellow leaf, I loved her—God knows how well!" He paused for a moment, evidently overcome by the retrospection he forced himself to face. What did he see? Alas! the pictures that floated before his mind's eye were like galvanized ghosts of the dead, whose faces were covered, by the coffin-lid. With a sigh, that was almost a sob, he turned from those bitter memories, and continued: "The usual game of cross purposes was played out. *She loved you.* So far all was well. You were a younger, fitter man than *I.* After all, I had never spoken; I had only loved, I had never thought of *marrying* the child— of gathering her spring into my dull autumn days. Well, she married you. I stood before the altar, and gave her to you with all my heart. Her happiness was my sole desire; so she was happy, *I* was content. What followed then? She disappeared for six long years from my eyes, from her world, from our world. We heard from chance acquaintances that you were seen here or there travelling, now in this place, now in that, but no direct word from *her* or *you*. So time passed. One morning I took up a foreign paper casually, and there read the news of your death somewhere in the East. Whether that announcement was inserted by accident or design, I know not. Whether you desired to relieve yourself of all responsibility for her whose life you had ruined, whose little fortune you had squandered, you best know. A paragraph stated that your wife, then your widow, was living somewhere in France. I set myself the task of searching for her, determining to solve the mystery that had shrouded her from her wedding-day. At last—you know where and how—I found her." He leaned forward, laid a hand on Lemaire's arm, and glared upon his face with an intensity of hatred and of horror that, hardened though he was, made him for a moment quail beneath his eyes.

"I know," he answered, sullenly. "I put her there for safety. She was mad!"

"Mad!" echoed Mr. Fleming, with bitter emphasis that defies description. He seemed shaken by a storm of passion, which he found it hard to control; dark thunder-clouds gathered in his eyes, and if the light-ning could have leaped forth, it would have scathed or slain his companion on the spot. "Mad!" he repeated once more. "No—but unnerved, terrified, heart-broken, cowed by your course of cruelty. I don't know by what devilry you succeeded in placing her there. I only know that, having squandered the little fortune she then possessed, you left her there neglected, forgotten, for four long years, and there your child was born."

"I knew nothing of that," exclaimed Lemaire. " I swear I knew nothing of that till long afterwards."

" She was nearly four years old," continued Mr. Fleming, "when I discovered them, and after much difficulty and many formalities I succeeded in releasing, and brought them away. My poor little Clara! I hardly knew her; so broken in health, broken in spirit, with nerves all shattered, she was but the shadow of herself. *You* were, on due authority, reported dead, and *I* married her, brought them home, adopted your child as mine. For a few years you left us in peace, in blind security—your existence undreamed of and forgotten. The cloud was lifted from Clara's life; she slowly regained her health and spirits, and was once more happy and content. Then this money—this cursed money, with which the devil angled for your miserable soul then, is angling for it now—was left to her ; at her death to her child or children, failing them to her husband. Then, and not till then, you rose from the dead—burst like an evil spirit upon our happy, peaceful home, and claimed your wife—*my* wife and child ! " (Both men grew suddenly ashen pale, as though they lived that terrible time over again.) " You threatened her with the law —nay, worse than the law, you threatened her with *yourself !* Man, you killed her ! as though you had struck her with an open knife. She died from the shame—shame at least in the world's eyes—of her position, the horror and dread of what might be to come. You threatened her with all the horrors of judge and jury, the criminal bar,

where she should stand on trial for bigamy
—into which, as I know now, you let her
drift. She could not live to face the scandal
and the shame. Man, I say again, *you*
killed her!"

"This is all long past," said Lemaire,
harshly; "it is no use uncovering old
wounds. I may have made some mistakes,
and had my failings as a man, but that does
not prevent my having feelings as a father!
Let bygones be bygones; I only ask for
what is right and fair—the custody of my
own child."

"Your child!" echoed Mr. Fleming,
bitterly. "Your cruelty shadowed her life
before she was born. She suffers from—
but there I will tell you nothing of her, and
I would sooner trust her to the mercies of
a wild beast than to *you.*"

"Nevertheless, in spite of any crotchet
of yours, I shall have her and take her with

me to the South. You insinuate that she
is delicate, and the trip will do her good;
Come, you know the law is on my side, and
I shall take legal steps to obtain possession
of my child. She is under age—I reminded
you of that before."

"And I answer as before," replied Mr.
Fleming, deliberately. "Under your care
she might not live to come of age."

"You dare to insinuate that in my hands
her life would be in danger?"

"Well, something like that I do plainly
insinuate," replied Mr. Fleming. "I believe
that in your love of greed there is nothing
you would not do; in your eagerness to
grasp the fortune which will be yours upon
her death—I speak plainly—you might be
led to hasten it."

M. Lemaire seemed in no way to feel
the natural indignation which such an
insinuation might be supposed to awaken;

but he answered with an unruffled countenance—

" You speak impressively, as though you were stating a fact; but you are getting an old man, Mr. Fleming, full of freaks and fancies. I cannot be held responsible for your insane ideas. You have no ground for your suspicions, no proof of any kind against me. If your charge or many charges against me were sifted, they would fall to the ground for want of evidence. The law can only deal with proven facts; it has nothing to do with morbid notions such as yours."

At this moment Jack unceremoniously sauntered into the room.

"Excuse the interruption, my dear Uncle," he said, " but has not this interview lasted almost long enough? Under too much excitement your invalid friend might have a relapse, you know."

Jack's entrance acted like a spell on M. Lemaire; he held his breath and absolutely gasped for a second, as though he had received a blow. Quick as a flash a light broke upon his mind, a suspicion entered his brain.

"Ah! I remember now," he exclaimed, as Jack stopped speaking. "You are young Jack Swayne! I see, I understand now your devotion to my child," he added, turning to Mr. Fleming. "I know now why you have kept her secluded from the world. You mean to enrich your family with the wealth that should be *mine*—to give my Clarice, your adopted daughter— ah! ah! I declare it sounds quite idyllic— to this man, your adopted son!"·

"Be good enough to leave me out of the question," said Jack, the danger-signal kindling in his eyes. "I don't allow people to take liberties with my name. I am not so squeamish as my uncle, and—I don't say I should—but I might be tempted to send you flying out of that window, and——"

"M. Lemaire is my guest—Jack, remember that," said Mr. Fleming, laying a deprecating hand upon his nephew's arm.

"A fact I cannot be called upon to remember, when he forgets it."

"With my own good-will I would never have crossed this accursed threshold," exclaimed M. Lemaire, furiously. "I would as soon have been the guest of the devil!"

"That may be a pleasure to come. Rest easy—he will give you a warm welcome one day!" said Jack, coolly smiling.

"Meanwhile"—interrupted Mr. Fleming, evidently anxious to stop the progress of any conversation between his cool-seeming but hot-tempered nephew and M. Lemaire; he felt that matters were slipping out of his own hand, and it might be out of his power to control them—"I don't believe there is any reason for prolonging this interview; all that we have to say has been said."

"True," exclaimed M. Lemaire, "talking is done with; I have now only to *act*, and act I think I shall to your confusion."

"I shall be ready to meet you on any ground you choose," said Mr. Fleming, with irritating dignity. "Your only reason for coming to Penally—so I understand you—was to claim Clarice; well, I absolutely refuse to give her into your custody, or to let you know where she is. Appeal to the law—but I do not think you will *dare* to lay your life open to inquiry. Do your best or your worst, I am prepared! Now, M. Lemaire, you are answered."

"Just one parting word of advice," said Jack. "I would advise you not to be found at any future time loitering in this neigh-bourhood; for my uncle's keepers are generally abroad, and—they carry guns, and you might meet with an accident. Occasionally I take a gun myself and go in for the wholesale slaughter of vermin—you know mistakes will sometimes happen."

Jack's presence acted upon M. Lemaire's nerves like a red rag on a mad bull; he grew furious, and poured forth a volley of threats and invectives. When people have poor arguments on their side, they can always take refuge in a storm of wild words. Presently he paused to take breath, and glared irefully upon the two men, who remained unmoved by his wild ravings. Jack, whistling an operatic air, looked out of the window, while Mr. Fleming sat silent with closed lips as though he had said the last word he meant to utter.

· " How you must love the sound of your own voice!" exclaimed Jack, during the momentary pause; " when you have quite

finished amusing yourself with this strong
language, perhaps you will let me have the
pleasure of driving you to the station—the
carriage is at the door."

At this juncture Hans made his appearance with M. Lemaire's overcoat and
travelling-bag; which had been forwarded
to the Manor House soon after his arrival
there. M. Lemaire felt that it would be
wise to take the hint, and close the interview. It had not ended so satisfactorily
as he had hoped it would; and he went.
away no wiser than he came, so far as the
chief object of his visit was concerned. He
saw, from the general aspect of affairs, that
he had better retire from the scene with
what dignity he could. Turning a look of
suppressed fury upon Mr. Fleming, he said—

"I wish you a good day, Mr. Fleming;
our next meeting will be in another place,
and will not end—like this." Mr. Fleming

bent his head, but uttered not a word. M. Lemaire added, "If I were strong enough I would walk to the station. If you will be good enough I should prefer that your man should drive me," he continued, darting a look of hatred at Jack ; "I am in no mood for company."

"Couldn't think of it!" exclaimed the imperturbable Jack. "For some days I have been looking forward to this pleasure, and I am sure you wouldn't wish to deprive me of it. Don't be afraid ; I shall not trouble you with much conversation. I shall smoke ; you can admire the landscape."

He kept his word, and left M. Lemaire to his meditations. Somehow they seemed to have been expected at the station. M. Lemaire seemed to be the only passenger; though there were a few stragglers on the platform, their only object seemed to be straggling, and as M. Lemaire passed to

the booking-office they regarded him with
curious eyes. He took his ticket for
London, and with a mocking bow, but
never a spoken word, to Jack Swayne, he
placed himself in a first-class carriage.
Meanwhile a little bit of by-play was taking
place, which he omitted to notice. In fact,
the last hours at the Manor House had
been so exciting that he felt exhausted, too
worn-out, for anything ; he wanted quiet
and rest. He leaned back in his seat, and
tried to pull himself together. A venerable-
looking man, a clergyman evidently by his
dress and the generally grave benignity of
his demeanour, suddenly appeared upon the
scene. He and Mr. Swayne were evidently
well acquainted ; they shook hands cordially,
and after a few minutes' conversation he
sauntered along the platform, got into the
compartment, and seated himself opposite
to M. Lemaire.

CHAPTER XVI.

" HUGH."

AFTER a brief consultation with his uncle, Jack followed M. Lemaire by a late afternoon train to London; and Mr. Fleming, as soon as the house was well cleared, drove down to the village and fetched Clarice home.

"It is so nice to be back again, father dear," she exclaimed, as she nestled on a stool at his feet, her arms crossed upon his knees, on this their first evening together after her brief absence. "It seemed so strange and mysterious to be sent away just because a stranger was staying here. Won't you tell me something about him?" she added, lifting an inquiring look to his face.

" The details of a sick-room are not very interesting, my darling ; and you have been very happy away?" he added, anxiously.

" Everybody has been very kind to me," replied Clarice; " and I have tried to be always cheerful, and to take an interest in things I didn't care about. But it is so hard to be always trying to seem something different from what you are; somehow I felt like a fish out of water trying to walk on its tail."

" Still, on the whole you have been well, and—less nervous?" So he framed the question; he could not ask in plainer words. He scrutinized her face anxiously as he spoke.

" Perhaps—I suppose so," she answered. " Once or twice, when I felt those dreadful feelings you know of coming on," she added, speaking below her breath, " I was afraid

people might know, and think I was queer;
so I fought against them—I hardly know
how, but I did, and I frightened them away,
and nobody knew—nobody ever knew ! "

She closed her eyes and laid her head
upon his knee. He stroked her golden hair
silently, soothingly, for awhile. There was
comfort in what she had said. So she
could, under *strong* motive, control those
morbid fancies, the pre-natal curse that
clung to her, and marred the freshness
of her beautiful young life. There was a
possibility, since she could once control
them, that she might outgrow these alternate
attacks of depression and terror of things
that had no existence. His heart beat high
at the possibility, but he said nothing, made
no remark whatever upon the subject ; it
would be better that she should be unconsciously acted upon. Without preparation
the current of changeful circumstances, or

current of electricity, that has always such a subtle effect upon the nervous system of our human machinery, might banish the cobwebs that occasionally, and only occasionally, clouded her brain. After a few moments of that silence which to both was more eloquent than speech, he said—

" You are a brave, dear child, and the old dad is glad to have his darling home again!" She only purred in answer, and rubbed her cheek upon his hand with the dumb motion of a contented animal. " Are you quite contented here, my darling ? " he added ; " you would not like to leave Penally ? "

" Leave Penally ! " exclaimed Clarice, a startled look coming into her face. " No, I don't think I shall ever want to leave Penally."

" Nor I either," he answered, " except perhaps for a time, for a little change—if it were necessary."

"I don't see why it should be necessary," she rejoined. "It is a lovely place, and I am beginning to like the people. You know I never have liked people before, I have always avoided or been glad to get away from them; and Miriam, whom I did not at all like at first, is beginning to be quite a friend of mine."

"I can't say I care for any of the Spencers much," said Mr. Fleming; "the young fellow is the best of them."

"Hugh! Oh, of course!" exclaimed Clarice, as though there could not be a doubt about it.

"Hugh!" repeated Mr. Fleming. "My dear child, how long is it that you have learned to call gentlemen by their Christian names?"

"Only since three days ago, dad dear," she answered, "when he asked me to. And I like it—it is not so formal as Mr. Spencer;

and when one knows people very well, one doesn't care to be formal."

" But I thought young Spencer was not coming back till late autumn."

" But he has," she answered quickly; "he arrived at the Rectory on Friday last. I don't think they expected him, but he came—and they were not particularly glad to see him."

"And how do you know that?" he inquired, seeming much interested.

" Miriam told me."

"Ay! So you've been keeping up a brisk correspondence with the Rectory people?" he observed.

"Yes, especially since Hugh's been home," she answered. " He came to see Miss Parkes every day, and always brought her fruit or flowers, or something he thought she would like to have."

" Called to see Miss Parkes every day ! " he repeated, with elevated brows.

"Wasn't it kind of him?" said Clarice; "and every evening too he dropped in, and I used to sing for him, and sometimes we sang duets together."

"Also for Miss Parkes's benefit!" he interrupted, with a touch of satire which, however, escaped her notice, "to cultivate her taste for music!"

"She generally slept through it," laughed Clarice, "and accompanied us with such snorts and gasps and growlings as I never heard, except when Katrina's taking forty winks."

"And the Doctor, did he go to sleep too?" inquired the old man, smiling as though he quite appreciated the situation.

"Ah! there was never any music when *he* was at home," she answered; "he calls it a 'noise,' and says it disturbs him—he can't think or do anything while it is going on." She paused a second, then added, "It is quite a treat to sing to Hugh, he not only *loves* music, but he feels it, and appreciates and sympathizes with the spirit of it—so different from other people. You know, darling, neither you nor Jack *really* care for music."

"How can you say that," said the old man, reproachfully, "when we make you sing to us every night!"

"Because you love *me*, and you know that I love it," replied Clarice. "But I always notice that music acts as a lullaby and sends you to sleep; and Jack looks so bored I sometimes get quite vexed, and vow to myself that I'll never afflict him with another note. But I can't help it: music is a part of me, and seems to carry me on its invisible wings to another world, and I am so surprised to find myself back in this. Jack doesn't understand that. With Hugh it is altogether different."

"You seem to have had a very pleasant time," said the old man, cheerily, though with a slightly troubled spirit. "You and young Spencer appear to have got on very well together; you—like him?"

"Like him!" she echoed; "do I?" she added, as though the idea had only just occurred to her. "Well, I don't know, but I suppose I do."

Mr. Fleming smiled and pinched her cheek, as he said, half jokingly—

"But not as you like Jack?"

"Oh no! in quite a different sort of way. Dear old Jack," she added, smiling affectionately, "he is always so good! Ah, what delightful rambles we used to have—he and Hugh, and Miriam and I; we were quite a pleasant *partie carrée.*"

Mr. Fleming smiled contentedly. He had been half inclined to be jealous of Hugh in a vicarious sort of way, but Clarice's frankness, the absence of confusion and self-consciousness, reassured him, and he was content. He knew so little of women. He knew nothing of the art of self-deception which nature teaches them to practise in such blind, innocent unconsciousness that, before they are well aware of it, they are lost in an intricate love-maze, where many wiser heads and stronger hearts have been lost before them.

Very happily venerable age and beautiful youth spent together their first hours of re-union. Clarice amused him with the daily history of her life since she had been away from home. Although they had held daily communication with each other, there was still so much to tell. She had grown quite fond of the genial Doctor, and looked with tender eyes upon the peculiarities of his sister, whose heart was good, though inordinate vanity held its stronghold in her

elderly brain, and sent her common sense
astray. Somehow the name of "Hugh,"
varied with the occasional introduction of
Miriam, cropped up oftener than Mr. Fleming quite approved.

In the course of conversation Clarice
made some few inquiries concerning his
late guest. His answers were so vague that
she could not help feeling that there was a
sort of concealment and reticence about Mr.
Fleming that was not the result of chance,
and was most unusual with him, for as a
rule there had always been a perfectly harmonious confidence between them—the rule
was broken now. More than once he was
on the verge of taking her fully into his
confidence and telling her all that had
taken place. Then he remembered the terror
that had been born with her—that her baby
brain had been shaken by an undefined
dread of something; then her fears had

taken shape, and she had learned too from
her mother's experience to dread the father
who had been no father. This dread lest
her child should suffer as she had suffered
had impelled the unhappy mother on her
death-bed to extract that promise from Mr.
Fleming which he resolved at any price to
hold sacred.

If Clarice were to know that M. Lemaire
had actually come to Penally to demand her
custody, had stayed at the Manor House
and breathed the atmosphere of her home,
she might feel that he had left the impress
of his presence in the air; for surely, since
disease clings to the walls, and floats subtly
and invisibly in the air we breathe, may not
an evil presence linger there likewise, and
reveal itself in some mysterious way through
the senses, especially when the mind is
prepared and ready to receive such an influence? He therefore felt that the facts, if

they came to her knowledge, might have an adverse effect upon her mind—just at this time, too, when he fancied that her nature was undergoing a kind of healing change, and her spirit slowly lifting itself out of the world of shadows into a purer, healthier light.

So, after giving the matter due consideration, he resolved to keep his own counsel, and let her remain in happy ignorance. Thus the ill-omened gap in their lives was bridged over, and the tide of the days and hours once more rolled calmly on. They resumed their old habits, and wandered along the seashore, and among the low-lying rocks when the tide was out, hunting for the specimens so dear to the old man's heart. Their close companionship was as tender and loving as it had always been, but something told him that his companionship was not so all-sufficient for the young girl as it had hitherto been. It seemed as though she was not able to settle back in the old life in the old way; there was a vague sense of unrest about her, a blind reaching out for something that was not there. She wandered about with Mr. Fleming, and ministered to him in sundry little ways as she had always done, but she did the familiar things not in the old familiar way; there was a preoccupation about her that at last attracted his attention.

"I am afraid you feel the Manor House a little lonesome after the Doctor's bustling household, my pet," he said one evening, as she seemed more listless and preoccupied than usual. "You seem to have had a lively time there, and perhaps you feel the change?"

"Well," she answered, reluctantly, "I suppose it is a kind of reaction; but I do feel a little dull sometimes, not the old dead

dulness, something quite different. I seem
to be listening for something I cannot hear,
looking for things that never come. You
see we have been so used to have Jack
about the place, I dare say his being away
makes a difference."

"I'll send for him," said the old man,
eagerly, fancying the very shadow of the
straw told him which way the wind was
blowing; "he was loth to go, and will be
only too glad to come back."

"No, no! not for the world!" exclaimed
Clarice, alarmed at the spirit her light words
had evoked; "but I think I should like—
if you wouldn't mind," she added quickly—
"to ask Miriam to come and spend a week
with me."

"My dear child, I shall be delighted!" he
answered readily. "Pray write and ask her
to come at once! I always thought the
society of young people was exactly what

you wanted, and now you are beginning to find it out yourself."

She answered nothing for a moment, but seemed to be reflecting; then she said in a low voice—

" I can't quite understand myself, but I shall be glad to have Miriam here. But, dad darling," she added, stealing her arms lovingly about his neck, " you don't mind? you don't think I'm ungrateful, or that I care the less for you because I am beginning to care a little for other people? I shall always love you best of all the world—you are more to me than any father ever was to any child. I could never do enough, never be enough."

" Tut, tut, my darling, you make my old eyes water ! " he answered, with a tender caress. " Why, you are the joy and comfort of my life ! But as for loving me the best of all the world !—no, no, that would be

unnatural, and I don't expect it. I hope
you will some day be happy in a better—at
least not a better, but a different kind of
love. I should be glad—you don't know how
glad—to give you into a true love's keeping;
for I am an old man, darling, older than my
years, and I have a presentiment that my
days are fast fading, and I have not long to
live; and I am called upon to set my house
in order."

"Don't, don't!" she exclaimed, shivering as though his words had struck upon
her naked soul. "Why will you talk so,
when you know how wretched it makes
me? What would become of your poor
Clarice? How could she live without
you?"

Mr. Fleming had not intended to give a
sombre turn to Clarice's thoughts, but he re-
traced the false step as quickly as he could.

"Well, well," he rejoined, quite cheerfully, "we must not meet troubles half-way. God is good, and I dare say will let me live as long as you want me."

"Then you will live as long as I do!" she exclaimed, smiling through the tears that, like an April shower, had gathered in her eyes.

Then he skilfully guided the conversation into a brighter channel: they talked of Miriam's visit, and what they should do to amuse her when she came. He knew how Clarice loved the sea, and suggested that perhaps Jack might be induced to bring his yacht, the *Firefly*, round, and take them for a cruise in the Mediterranean; indeed, he had long ago half promised to organize some such little trip—as poor Miriam fancied, for *her* pleasure.

When Katrina attended her young mistress that evening, she thought that for many a day she had not seen her look so blooming

nor in such cheerful spirits. There was a
soft light shining in her eyes, dimpled smiles
rippled over the lovely face, and the very
blood seemed coursing through her veins to
a joyful tune. The old nurse lingered longer
than usual over Clarice's golden tresses,
combing and combing with a sort of drowsy
precision, as though she was trying to mes-
merize the brain, and coax it to give up any
of the fancies or wild imaginings that might
be entangled there, that through them she
might learn the why and the wherefore of
the change that had come over her. But
the brain kept its own secret, and the sweet
lips told her nothing. Before they parted
Clarice kissed the old lady on both cheeks,
saying—

"Good-night, Katrina dear. I feel as
though we were leaving our dark days behind us and going to find a new world, a
new sun! We will have a gay summer now.

Good-night. I'm quite tired; I want to sleep."

Did she sleep? Ah! who can tell? Who can trespass on a maiden's slumbers, or follow her through the shadowy land of dreams!

CHAPTER XVII.

LOVE'S YOUNG DREAM.

THE next morning, just as they were sitting down to breakfast, a letter was handed to Mr. Fleming.

"From the Rectory, sir; and the messenger waits for an answer," said Hans.

"Say that I'll be there in less than an hour," exclaimed Mr. Fleming, as he glanced through the epistle; "and Hans, order the horses round at once, that I may start as soon as I have finished breakfast."

"What is the matter, father dear?" inquired Clarice.

"Nothing of any consequence, my child,"

he answered—"nothing, at least, that closely concerns us. I fancy that military hero, Ben, has got into some trouble."

"Poor old Ben, he's always getting into hot water—I think he suffers from Tel el Kebir on the brain," said Clarice, as she proceeded leisurely to pour out the coffee. "Don't hurry, dear, you know it always gives you indigestion; and the business— Ben's business, at least—will not spoil by a few minutes' delay."

They proceeded leisurely with their breakfast. The sea-breeze, laden with its fresh briny odours, swept in through the open window; the air was filled with the song of birds and the drowsy hum of the industrious bees, on their honey-seeking wanderings; the flowers nodded their plumed heads in at the window, their mute perfumed lips breathing a welcome to her who loved them: they had not been neglected during her absence—the gardener had given them water when they were thirsty and looked · after them in a general way, but it was a rough way, different from her loving, tender care. She regarded her flowers as sentient things that could feel a kind touch, and shivered and shrank from rough handling; for even the thirsty flowers are more refreshed by the delicate draught daintily given, than by a whole bucket full of water flung over them just to keep them from dying. The dumb, still life that gives so much and takes so little, is a ceaseless and pathetic appeal to our human affections.

It was a pretty home-picture. Bouncer was seated, tall and erect, by his mistress's side, his faithful eyes fixed upon her face, and the many thumps of his tail upon the floor told her how glad *he* was to be home again. He had had rather a hard time at Miss Parkes's, being constantly irritated by

the presence of her favourite tabby " Griselda." Of course Bouncer knew well enough
that puss was on her own ground, and had
the best right there; but conscientious
scruples cannot always be expected to hold
with the best of dogs, and in some secret
occult fashion Bouncer made inroads upon
Griselda's peace of mind : he forced her
from her stronghold upon the hearthrug,
where she had blinked and dozed through
her kittenish days, and even when she took
refuge in her mistress's work-basket, harried
her from that abode of bliss. At last things
broke out into a state of open warfare. One
day, loud barking and feline cursing and
swearing were heard in the library, and
Bouncer was discovered in a state of furious
excitement, making frantic attempts to
reach Griselda, who had sprang to the top
of the bookcase, and sat there swelling out
of all proportion, spitting and hurling down

smothered curses on her enemy. As a rule
this kind of affair was beneath Bouncer's
dignity—all other minor animals were safe
from him; but a cat! it was not in human
—I mean not in canine nature to lie down
with such an enemy. Bouncer was caught
red-handed, with his mouth full of Griselda's
fur, and was at once relegated to the stable.

"I'm sorry to send him out of the house,
my dear, as you are so fond of him," apolo-
gized Miss Parkes; "but he's a dangerous
beast; he'll be best in the stable—if he
worries the horses they'll kick his brains
out."

Clarice felt and expressed great sorrow
for poor Griselda, and herself conveyed
Bouncer to his place of punishment, talking
to him reproachfully by the way, trying to
show him what a bad, wicked dog he had
been; but though he hung his head and
looked ashamed, he was unrepentant; there

was a look of cat-i-cide in his eye which told what he would do if he had another opportunity. He felt the degradation of his position keenly, as any dog of self-respect and dignity would do; but there was no help for it—to the stables he must go, and sleep on straw like a poor parish casual. Well, the evil days were over now —they were all at home once more.

The meal progressed, eggs were cracked, toast demolished, and even the morning paper spelt over before they rose from the table, when Clarice said suddenly, as though the idea had just occurred to her—

"May I go with you to the Rectory? I think I should enjoy the drive, and I could give Miriam a personal invitation: that would be nicer than writing—and, who knows, perhaps Miriam may come back with us."

"If you think that likely, you had better

have your ponies out," said Mr. Fleming. "I've heard Miss Spencer say she objected to drive in a two-wheeled vehicle."

"Ah, yes, she was thrown out once, and that naturally gave her a scare," said Clarice; "so perhaps we had better have the ponies."

"Then make haste and get ready; I should like to start at once."

Clarice was soon hatted and gloved, and the ponies trotted off through the beautiful still morning air, with the sea stretching away on the one side, lost in the misty purple-tinted clouds that rested on the horizon, and the soft swelling hills and wooded wonders with all their leafy wonders on the other.

They soon reached the Rectory, and were at once ushered into the study, where the Rector himself was installed with all the virtues of stern inexorable justice throned upon his brow. In a small adjoining room, waiting the reverend gentleman's leisure, was the delinquent Ben, in custody of the rural policeman, who had found him in the wood before daybreak, and in his possession two rabbits and a hare, which he admitted he had obtained on the Manor House grounds.

"My dear Mr. Fleming," said the Rector, shaking hands cordially with his neighbour, "I am sure you will excuse my sending for you in this informal way, but I want you to see for yourself with what base ingratitude that fellow Ben repays your kindness. Over-consideration and generosity to this sort of people are a mistake. If you remember I have suggested something of the kind to you—now I'm going to show you an example of it."

"I'm sorry to hear it, for Ben is rather a *protégé* of mine," said Mr. Fleming; "I

don't think he has been kindly dealt with
—that's why I always take his part."

" Ah," exclaimed the Rector, with a
satisfied grunt, " and you've *protégéd* him
to some purpose."

He summoned the occupants from the
next room, and in another moment policeman X Y 2 appeared upon the threshold,
looking, and swelling with official dignity,
as pompous as the Rector's self; beside him,
with a sullen downcast expression of countenance, stood Ben, loaded with his unlawful
spoils.

" There ! " exclaimed the Rector, triumphantly, addressing Mr. Fleming, and evidently expecting horror and indignation to
take possession of his venerable countenance,
" see how you have been deceived. You
thought you had put that fellow in the way
of getting an honest living : see how he
carries out your idea—by poaching on your

own grounds and literally robbing his bene-
factor! Well, what have you got to say
for yourself? "—this roughly to Ben.

" I don't want to say nothin' at all,"
snarled Ben, with a furtive glance at Mr.
Fleming's face, as though to see how he
was likely to regard the affair; " and if
anybody's hard-up for want of a rabbit, I'll
give 'em up."

" No insolent levity here, sir," said the
Rector, with a vindictive snap. " I'll stop
your snaring propensities for the future,
and send you to gaol for the longest period
the law allows."

" One moment," exclaimed Mr. Fleming;
" is it with this offence only you are deal-
ing ? "

" Only with this at present," replied the
Rector, rubbing his hands gleefully; " but
I dare say if we give him a chance——"

" But I don't want to give him a chance,"

interrupted Mr. Fleming, "and I am not
so sure that this is an offence after all.
The fact is, though you may not be aware
of it, I have given leave to some of our
poorer neighbours to relieve me of a few
rabbits now and then. There are thousands
running wild about my place, and they do
a great deal of damage; I am rather glad
to get rid of them. But I think you ought
to be contented with one at a time, Ben,"
he added, reproachfully.

"But, my dear sir," gasped Mr. Spencer,
"you don't understand that this is a case
of poaching—not so much an offence against
you, as against the *Law*, and you have not
the right to condone it."

"My dear friend, you need not fear my
stepping an inch beyond my right," answered
Mr. Fleming; "but where there is no wrong
committed there can be no condonation,
and I certainly have the right to give my

poorer neighbours the liberty of taking a few rabbits off my grounds."

" But *have* you given this man the right?" inquired the Rector.   .

" I am not on oath," said Mr. Fleming, smiling, " and I cannot swear to trifling facts; but I have given a kind of general permission, and I dare say Ben so understood it."

" Of course I did," said the mendacious Ben; " I don't think much o' laws, as a rule, but I wouldn't go agin Mr. Fleming—no, not for ten thousand rabbits."

" Do you really wish the fellow to get off scot-free, after so grossly trespassing on your property ? " inquired the amazed Rector.

" I don't admit the trespass, and I do wish him to go free," replied Mr. Fleming, decidedly.

" Then let him go, policeman," said the Rector. " Be off, Ben—you've escaped this

time by the skin of your teeth ; if I had my
will I'd commit you for ten days."

"Better luck next time, sir," exclaimed
Ben, grinning from ear to ear; "dessay
yer'll find some poor hungry cretur pulling
a carrot stump or a turnip to keep her from
starving—yer can enjoy yerself then, yer
know, and give her double. It's a pity yer
can't have folks flogged as well as gaoled—
wouldn't yer enjoy seeing the blood fly!"
He gathered up his spoils ; he made a most
reverential obeisance to Mr. Fleming.
"You're a gentleman, you are, sir, and if
ever yer want a man as 'ud swear away his
life for yer, here's one as 'ud do it."

This flattering offer was received in silent
deprecation by Mr. Fleming, and a look of
intensified condemnation hurled from the
Rector's reverend brow.

When the two gentlemen were left alone,
the conversation naturally rising out of the

foregone interview turned upon the game laws, which they discussed in a lively characteristic fashion ; and the Rector tried to convince Mr. Fleming that by his wrong-headed leniency he was helping Ben, and others of that ilk, on their way to the gallows, but somehow he didn't seem to believe it.

" Besides, my dear friend," added the Rector, " consider your neighbours, who one and all feel very strongly on the point ; you will have the whole county in a blaze if you allow this sort of thing."

" I am sorry," he answered, " but I cannot square my conscience to *my neigh-bours'* rule of right. I must act on my own responsibility as they on their."

" But you know coursing has always been such a favourite sport, and if everybody followed your example, where would it be ? Why nowhere ! "

"And I don't think humanity would suffer very much from the want of it. I think it would be quite as well if some few other manly sports—pigeon-shooting among them—were banished into 'nowhere.' At any rate, I'm not disposed to preserve that sort of game for the rich while my poorer neighbours are starving."

"What very odd notions you have, my dear friend," rejoined the Rector; "I see it is no use to argue the matter."

"It would be rather a waste of time," said Mr. Fleming, smiling, "and I really think we might be better employed in paying our respects to the ladies, for instance. I brought Clarice over with me, and I think she is trying to persuade Mrs. Spencer to allow your daughter to come on a visit to the Manor House for a few days."

Meanwhile the ladies had been arranging their own business; the invitation had been cordially given and graciously accepted; for, in spite of Mrs. Spencer's often-uttered animadversions on "the Manor House people," she never lost an opportunity of cultivating their acquaintance, and was delighted that her daughter Miriam should be invited on a visit there. Who could tell what insight into forbidden mysteries she might obtain? or what crumbs of gossip she might gather together to feed the hungry maws of the curious, whose early awakened appetites were still unsatisfied, and the game of speculation was still being carried on—and somehow with redoubled interest since M. Lemaire's advent.

"The whole of the proceedings at that time were strange, to say the least of it"—so everybody said; the least light thrown upon the subject would be eagerly welcomed. The injured man's very name was unknown. He had been thrown wounded into their midst, and accordingly he was everybody's property; each felt that individually they had a vested interest in him. But the Manor House had taken possession of him, and then hustled him out of the village without giving any one a chance of a word with him. Those who could speak, Dr. Parkes and Mr. Fleming, were both absolutely dumb.

So Miriam and her healthy appetite went off to the Manor House next day, and it was not difficult for the mother's heart to speculate on the probability of Hugh's frequently transferring himself and his alarming hunger to the same place; which domestic arrangement would be greatly beneficial to the Rectory larder, which had suffered severely from his wolfish attacks—it was always empty.

There quickly began a new reign of pleasant days and hours at the Manor

House; and Hugh, as well as Miriam, became almost domiciled there, for never a day passed without his making his appearance during some part of it. He quite won Mr. Fleming's heart, too, by the interest he took in his specimens; he made himself useful in many ways, and spent whole hours in the *sanctum*, assisting in the arranging and cataloguing of his collection, and enlivened the somewhat monotonous routine by telling lively anecdotes of things he had heard and people he had known, all more or less interesting or laughable. Everything reminded him of something else; in the midst of the most dry-as-dust proceeding he would burst out in his hearty, genial way, " By the bye, that reminds me, etc.," and he rushed off into some wild, improbable story, for the truth of which he was ready to vouch on a " mile of bibles; " and the old man felt that his studies had never been so pleasant, nor his labours so lightened, as when Hugh Spencer shared them.

So it fell out that he grew to look for the young man's coming, and to fret and chafe if he were delayed for a few hours; he wanted to show him this, or consult him about that; in fact Hugh was always in demand, and he could not settle down to his "labour of love" until he came. So things arranged themselves pleasantly for all parties, and somehow it became a habit for Hugh to stay to dinner; then came the pleasant twilight hours, when the old man indulged in his after-dinner nap, and Miriam, who was not musical, betook herself with her shaded lamp and her embroidery to the other end of the room, and Hugh coaxed Clarice—who did not need much coaxing, by the bye—to sit down to the piano and play to him snatches of dreamy melodies, and sometimes they sang together in soft, low voices through the drowsy twilight. One evening they lingered thus longer than usual, till the twilight had died away, and the crescent moon, outlined sharp and clear as a silver scythe, shone from the dark-blue skies, and sent its pale beams wandering through the dusky air till they glided into the room where they were seated and kissed Clarice's hands, and touched her golden hair with a silvery light. Mr. Fleming still slept, and Miriam still bent over her embroidery, sending the needle in and out with the monotonous precision that is so irritating to the nerves of the idle looker on. Clarice stopped playing, and let her hands fall idly in her lap.

" Come out for a turn on the terrace— do; it is such a lovely night ! " Hugh whispered softly in her ear.

" I always enjoy an evening stroll," she smiled in answer, "and I always have it too—no matter what the weather is ; indeed I rather like a ramble on a stormy night, when the sea seems full of strange voices, and the wind moans and blows us hither and thither, and the rain comes pelting in our faces—the very struggle to keep our feet is a delightful sensation."

"But surely such a night as this——" he began.

" Oh, these nights are well enough, but I like the wild weather best ; there is something in me that seems to understand and answer to the storm. Come, Miriam," she added, quickly, throwing a lace mantle over her head.

" Thanks, dear — I'm tired," Miriam answered ; "I've been walking the greater part of the day. Besides, I want to finish this piece of work ; I've been lazy long enough ; if I don't stick to it, it will never be done.''

So Hugh and Clarice passed out together. The twilight shadows lay upon the landscape, shrouding its features so that trees, shrubs, and flowers were merely blurred and blotted outlines, leaving nothing distinct. On the one side they knew the sea, with its living world of mysteries, was stretching away beyond the limit of the land out of their sight, veiled in a grey mist like a valley of shadows, but they could hear its soft lullaby as it ran rippling along the shore. The two paced slowly up and down, listening with their spirits' ears to other tales than the whispering wind or wandering waves could tell them. Neither spoke much, only now and then a few low uttered words, that in the dreamy silence sounded like a caress, and that was all. A silence that was more eloquent than speech brooded over them, and drew them together, and held them fast in its invisible magic bonds. So, enjoying the sweet luxury of silence, they stepped like noiseless shadows side by side through the dusky night. The crescent moon had slowly faded, and above their heads the deep blue skies were abloom with golden stars, and among them long trailing feathery clouds were floating.

Clarice had never thought or speculated about love; she had known no maidenly hopes or fears or wonderment at all. She only felt that when Hugh was by the whole aspect of the world was changed. His presence made all the difference to her, brought light where there was darkness, and set her life dimpling with sunshine and gladness. When he was by, time flew " swift as the swallow's flight;" when he was absent, it hobbled as though its winged feet were hampered with a leaden clog.

Presently she sat down, filled with a tremulous joy and most sweet content, and he placed himself beside her under the flickering shadow of the silver birch. Somehow his hand took possession of hers, and his arm softly circled her supple waist, and she became conscious that a pair of passionate eyes were gazing into the chaste depths of hers, and a voice, his voice, sounding to her as in a dream, said softly—

"Clarice, you know I love you!" The floodgates of speech once opened, his long suppressed feelings found vent, and his first brief words were followed by a torrent of loving, passionate protestations. His arms were round her still; she made no effort to release herself from their embrace, but she answered nothing as he poured his living love, with all love's purest eloquence, into her ears. She remained motionless as a statue, as though she neither heard, saw, or felt. His revelation seemed to paralyze her senses, and woke no answer either from her heart or lips.

"My love! my lily bud! won't you speak?" he urged, anxiously, at last. He waited a moment; no word came, but he fancied the frail figure quivered slightly. "Is it—my God, is it that you *don't care?*" There was a ring of such intense pain in his voice that it forced her, with a kind of mesmeric power, to turn her face to his. Even beneath the starlight he saw that her face was radiant with something more than its own beauty, and her eyes were shining as through a mist that was not of sorrow. He saw—he knew—by some subtle telegraphy—she had no need to speak. In the sweet abandonment of a pure, innocent love, she let her arms fall about his neck.

"I do care," she murmured in a voice scarcely above a whisper. "Oh, Hugh!

my Hugh! I think I have loved you
always!"

The fair head drooped upon his breast,
and with a proud, passionate exultation,
that words could poorly express, he clasped
her close in his arms. She lifted her face,
and their lips met in one long, illimitable
kiss; and all the world, all the to-morrows,
all the kisses that might follow after, would
never wash away the memory of this one—
the firstborn of a sweet, pure love.

"Clarice! Clarice! where are you?
Come in, the dews are falling," exclaimed
a familiar voice, which brought them
straight down from heaven to earth. A
footstep sounded on the gravel; some one
was groping blindly towards them.

"Here we are, father dear," said a soft
voice from the shadows of the birch-tree;
and the two, who had climbed the heights
of human felicity, came tumbling down

from the cloudland of dreamy delights to face the commonplace of to-day. Their secret joy was already over, quietly passing away to rest amid the dead yesterdays.

CHAPTER XVIII.

THE next morning when Hugh arrived at the Manor House he found Clarice looking pale and shy and silent, returning only a quiet smile in answer to the greeting of his glad, passionate young eyes. Any observant looker-on must have read his story there as plainly as if it had been printed. Miriam saw it; she knew, and was glad—not perhaps quite unselfishly glad. We are all more rejoiced in our brother's fortune, if we can carry forward and set down some slight balance to our own account.

The lovers got no single word together

on Hugh's arrival, for Mr. Fleming at once
carried the young man off to his *sanctum*,
believing that in doing so he was paying
him the greatest possible compliment: it
was not everybody he would have trusted to
handle his butterflies and bluebottles. He
had some cause to find his confidence mis-
placed on the present occasion; for somehow Hugh's general intelligence seemed to
desert him. He was in his customary high
spirits, and was as amusing and chatty as
ever, but he handled things with a rough-
ness that made the old man tremble, and
he was cautioning him to " be careful " all
the time. Then he made a ridiculous mistake, and arranged the wing of a butterfly
to the body of a death's-head moth. With
much difficulty that was rectified. At last,
to crown all, in a state of demented felicity,
he sat down on a case of newly arranged
valuable specimens, and went crashing

through the insect world; and in one minute destroyed the labours of a week. Never did a bull in a china-shop do so much damage in so short a time!

Mr Fleming, in a horrified condition of mind—which courtesy towards his guilty guest led him to conceal as far as possible—awoke to the fact that his sagacious young friend was a little too much for him on this special morning; indeed there was altogether a reckless flightiness in his manner that was quite alarming, and, judging in all charity, Mr. Fleming fancied he had perhaps been smoking too much, or something worse; or perhaps these were only symptoms of an impending fever fiend! and mildly he suggested—

"I don't think you are very well this morning. You know things should be taken in time; it does not do to neglect early symptoms. There! there!" he added, in some alarm, seeing Hugh was about to attack a newly arrived treasure. " God bless my soul ! your pulse is going like a steam-hammer. I really think you had better go home and take a pill, or consult Dr. Parkes, and you may be all right to-morrow."

" I do feel a little queer," admitted Hugh, with a comical expression of countenance, rejoiced to receive his polite dismissal; " but a ramble through your beautiful woods will do me more good than a sack of pills or a whole army of doctors. *Au revoir !* You're sure I can do nothing more for you this morning ? "

Mr. Fleming frankly declined for the present : he considered he had done quite enough. As soon as Hugh's back was turned, he set himself to repair the mischief he had done. The young man rushed off in search of Clarice. He could not find her in the house ; but Miriam was in the morning-room,

torturing the piano out of its senses, playing
and practising in a dull, monotonous way, as
people do who have no music in their souls.
But she was conscientiously bound, by the
stern maternal law, to practise at least one
hour every day; and she did her duty.

"Well!" she exclaimed, as Hugh put
his head in at the door.

"Where's Clarice?" he inquired.

"Gone out. I wanted her to stay and
have a practise with me, but she wouldn't,"
answered Miriam, in a slightly aggrieved
tone.

"I should think not! Your style of practising would drive any real lover of music
mad," was his rejoinder.

"You needn't be rude;" and Miriam
banged away louder than ever.

"Did she say which way she was going?"
he asked, eagerly.

"No, and I don't think she expects you to

follow her. She said she wanted to talk to something or somebody who wouldn't answer back; so I suppose she has gone into the woods to have a pleasant conversation, and listen to the trees' dumb talk as the heathens used to do. She has got such queer ways—sometimes, I think, quite unchristian!"

Hugh had disappeared long before she came to the end of her speech. Being tolerably familiar with all her haunts, he knew pretty well where he would find Clarice, and hurrying through the wilderness, he soon caught sight of her light skirts fluttering among the trees. In a few minutes he was beside her, holding her two hands in his, his glad young eyes feasting right royally on the lovely face. The great blue eyes that were lifted to his looked troubled and anxious, and the sensitive lips quivered slightly, even while they smiled.

"My lily love!" he exclaimed fondly;

" what, wandering here all alone with only your silent thoughts for company ? "

" But my thoughts are sometimes louder than other people's words," answered Clarice, " and they say so much more."

" You knew that I should come ! " said Hugh, his high-spirited, very human nature being utterly unable to answer a poetical idea except in the plainest prose. All the poetry in his nature was dumb; he could *feel* but not talk—while sometimes those who can talk do not feel at all. " That, like a living loadstone, wherever you went you would draw me after ! " he continued.

" Yes, I knew," she answered—" I felt you were coming ; my heart heard you, I think, long before you came."

" Little darling ! " exclaimed the delighted Hugh, gazing at her with loving admiration. " How prettily you say things ! Do you know I went home last night like a raving

maniac—kissed hands to the moon, shouted
to the winds and waves! I wanted everything to know how happy I was, and the
very stars seemed to wink down with a
million eyes, as though they knew all about
it, and quite agreed that the world held no
happier man than *I!* Oh, my love, my
very own!" he added, and a grave serious-
ness came into his voice, "I can hardly
believe that it is all really true! I fancy I
shall wake up and find it is all a dream,
and you have faded from my life like a mist
maiden! Last night seems so long ago!"

"Oh, Hugh! dear Hugh!" exclaimed
Clarice, lifting a pair of drowned blue eyes
to his, "I'm so sorry; I wish there had been
no last night! Can't you—don't you think
you can forget all about it?"

"Forget all about it!" echoed Hugh.
"I should rather think *not*. Why, after
we've been together fifty years, it will be as

fresh in my memory as it is to-day. My sweet, between you and me there will never be anything forgotten ! " he added, with an air of proud proprietorship.

" Oh, but there must, Hugh, there must ! It was all a mistake, all that was said last night. When you have heard all that I have to tell, you will see that it is no use—that it is wrong, almost a crime, for us to love one another ! And it is all my fault," she added, her voice trembling with emotion.

" My darling ! " he exclaimed, startled by her earnestness. " What can you mean— wrong ! crime ! and it is all your fault ! Why—but no, it is impossible ! you are not one of that sort." He stood still and held her before him, " Look me straight in the eyes, Clarice. Tell me, is there any one else—any other man ? " His stern, threatening look frightened her.

" Oh no ! no !—nobody but you ; there

never was—there never could be anybody but *you!*" Her tone, her look, satisfied—nay, more than satisfied him, as indeed it would have satisfied any man.

" Very well—then that's all right," he exclaimed, with a little premonitory squeeze. " You're a little nervous darling—afraid of the old gentleman perhaps? Well, I'll soon set things straight. I'll speak to him this very day ! "

" Speak to father ! No, you mustn't do that, Hugh," she said, decisively.

" To-morrow, then ? "

" No, not to-morrow—nor ever at all. We must keep silent—keep our own secret always, Hugh, between our two selves."

Hugh turned an amazed look on the earnest face, so almost childish in the innocent candour of its expression.

" But would that be fair ? " he observed. " It is best always to be straightforward, my

Clarice. The dear old man trusts me, and I could not come and go, carrying your love about with me—and *he* not knowing. Perhaps you think he'll object. Shouldn't be surprised if he did—I should in his place. But we must act on the square, my dear, and give him a chance," added the practical Hugh, magnanimously. " Don't be afraid ; I'm an obstinate brute, and not fifty fathers, with a hundred arms, moral, legal, or physical, should take my darling from me !" He illustrated his powers of possession on the spot, and imprisoned her as fast in his arms as though he never meant to let her go.

" But suppose it had nothing to do with the dear old dad, Hugh,! Suppose *I* took *myself* away ? "

" That's all bosh ! " said Hugh. " A woman can't give herself to a man one day and take herself away the next ; it's against nature. You gave yourself to me last night, and I'll hold you fast."

They walked on under the overhanging trees, with the sunlight glinting through their leafy branches, and dancing in a thousand fantastic shadows at their feet. As the pathway narrowed they had to walk single-file; he went first, lifting aside the troublesome branches for her to pass under them., Presently they came out upon an open space with mossy banks, gnarled lichen-covered tree trunks and low-growing bushes sloping downwards towards the shore. Here they sat down, their faces turned seaward, with the green screen of the woodland and background of purple hills rising behind them ; the seagulls, driven landward, wheeled in eddying circles above their heads, and the air was stirred with the last soft songs of the lingering summer birds.

It was a lovely lonely solitude, just the
kind of place and scene that Clarice most
delighted in ; but she was not disposed to
delight in any outward scene just now. She
looked round without seeing or feeling anything much, only fully awake to the one
fact—viz., that Hugh was beside her, her
hand close clasped in his, and—ah ! she knew,
without looking, exactly how his love-lighted
eyes were gazing on her downcast face. The
spell of the hour was upon her ; the one
beloved presence, the sun-god of her cloudy
life, was shining, wrapping her round as in a
glorified mantle, saturating her through and
through with a keenness of joy that was
akin to pain.

She sat silent as under a spell—and surely
love is the one true natural magic when it
reveals itself to a fresh, innocent young
spirit ! She was dumb, and felt as though
she would never care to speak again ; for the

words she spoke would break the spell
and disperse the sweet illusion for ever!
He was supremely happy too—he didn't
want to talk; he knew he was not good
at talking : and to him it was a kind of
intoxicating delight, to hold her soft little
hand in his, to feel they were together, and
to know that through their veins there
circulated the same love-poison ; and above
all was the supreme feeling that to this one
most fair woman *he* was "the all in all!"
Presently a few caressing words fell from his
lips.

"*Ma mie*, is not this lovely! Do you
know I should like to take you in my arms
this very minute, and float away with you
up among the clouds, and sail on and on
through all the worlds that are, and never
come back to this world again!"

"Ah! if we only could!" she answered,
nestling closer to his side and looking up in

his face with frank, loving eyes. " Hugh, I
know I'm selfish, wickedly selfish; but I'm
glad you love me ! glad you told me so ! and
I—but there, you will never know what
you are to me ! But, Hugh," she added,
looking down, and playing nervously with
the buttons of his coat, " would it hurt you
very much to say good-bye ? "

" Would it hurt me very much to have
my head cut off ? Yes, I think it would—
rather," he answered; " but I'm not likely to
try either experiment at present, thank you!"

" It would be best and wisest—indeed the
only thing that we can do : you will see that,
when I have told you——" She hesitated.

" Well, come, what have you got to say ?
Out with it—I hate beating about the bush.
But kiss me first, that I may have strength
to bear the fearful ordeal." Obedience to his
commands was shyly but promptly paid;
then he settled himself comfortably with his

arms round her, and her head nestling on his shoulder. Having arranged things to his satisfaction, he gave the word of command : " Now fire away ; my ears are stretched as long as asses'. Behold, I listen ! "

" It is like killing myself," she murmured, in a broken voice ; " I can't bear to tell you——"

"Then don't," interrupted he, philosophically ; " I'm not curious, and I only listen to please you."

" Did you ever hear, did anybody ever hint to you, that I was not quite like other people—a little queer sometimes ? " A strange, furtive look came into her eyes as she glanced up at him.

" Bless my soul, I always knew that ! " exclaimed Hugh, heartily. " I didn't want anybody to tell me ; I found that out for myself. My little queen ! thank God, you are not ' like other people.' "

"But you don't understand," she added, desperately. "I am not always as you have seen me: I have such terrible thoughts— am haunted with a dread of things that I shudder to speak of. And oh! Hugh! Hugh!" she cried out, with an anguish in her voice, "I think sometimes I'm a little —*mad!*"

"That is foolish, Clarice," he answered, gravely; "you shouldn't give way to such ideas. It is wrong; you don't know where they may lead you. I heard of a woman once who fancied she was a teapot, and— well she ended her days in a lunatic asylum at last."

"That is where I began!" she exclaimed, now grown ghastly pale, with all the light and love and sweetness dying out of her face. "That is where I began," she repeated in a dead, cold whisper—"and I dread lest I end there! I lived among

them! Ah, though I was but a little child
I remember it! Everything was upside
down. At night there were horrible screams.
Ah, I hear them now! and I—I am afraid!
Sometimes I have such terrible thoughts,
am hunted by such hideous, shapeless fears,
that I want to creep away under the earth
and hide away from myself. I can't tell
you—words are such poor things—but a
thousand wouldn't *tell* you what I feel in a
single minute! *You see I was born there!* "
she added, in the same freezing whisper,
which showed where lay the keynote of all
she felt, all she suffered. " Though my body
is away, and though I, this bodily me, walk
and talk, and eat and drink, like the rest of
the world, sometimes I think, What if they
have kept my soul *there*—if they sometimes
send it after me? And *then* I—oh! why
will you make me say it? Don't you understand now, that love, and all sweet things

that make life sweet to live, are *not for me!*"

"I don't understand anything of the kind," answered Hugh, who had listened to her very gravely. "It seems to me that love will be the best cure for your *maladie imaginaire.* I see how it is," he added, frowning, and feeling for the moment angry with all her surroundings; "you have been neglected, and allowed to brood on these things too much, till you have created a bugbear and are frightening yourself to death! The fact of being born in a madhouse doesn't make *you* mad! Of course it is not pleasant—naturally you would rather have been born somewhere else; but, as a mere matter of fact, it doesn't affect you at all. Why, if you'd been born in a stable do you think you'd have been a horse?"

The idea was not original, but it just occurred to him, and served to illustrate his meaning. The healthy, practical turn of his mind seemed in a way to affect her on the surface, for the moment at least— as a fresh breath of pure air will bring back the colour to the worn, wan cheek, and give it for a moment the glow of health. He talked to her reasonably, most lovingly, and there was a good stratum of common sense in all he said. He battled with and fought down the fiends of her delusive imagination, and, like a mental Jack the Giant Killer, he conquered, and his enemies—*her* enemies— lay dead at their feet; and for the time at least she came out of the land of shadows wherein she was so often lost, and stood on a level beside him in the fresh, wholesome air.

They wandered down to the shore and strolled on their way homeward by the sundown sea, while all the land was gorgeously aglow in the golden sunset. They watched the bright colours fade and mingle one with another till they settled into a solemn sombre grey, and sent the twilight shadows creeping earthward, shrouding all things with a tender mystery ; and through all the surrounding darkness the girl's spirit seemed to rise up and see the light.

Hugh inspired her with something of his own happy, hopeful spirit; she no longer looked as " through a glass darkly," but saw with a brighter, clearer vision. A part of his life seemed to enter into hers as he cheered and encouraged her, exorcising the demon despair, and setting in his place the angel of hope and promise. After all, the things she most dreaded were only " might be's ! " and with Hugh by her side—Hugh always with her, his precious love clasped to her heart of hearts—what ugly evil thought or fear could ever come near her ?

As they drew near the house, they met

Mr. Fleming and Miriam coming in search of them. One at least was surprised to find them together.

" By a lucky chance," exclaimed Hugh, " I met Miss Lemaire in the wood, and coaxed her to take a stroll by the sea. I hope you've not been alarmed ? "

" No," he answered, " Clarice enjoys a lonely ramble; she is used to come and go as she pleases, but—I am always a little anxious."

" Good night, my sweet! " were Hugh's whispered words as he parted from her some time afterwards. " Be brave and strong ! No more dark thoughts. Remember you hold my heart in your hand—if you hurt yourself you hurt me more. Shall you tell him to-night?" he whispered, as, with his arms round her, he gave her the " good night " kiss.

" No ! no ! " she exclaimed, shrinking from the responsibility.

" Then I shall be here to speak to him to-morrow."

A few more blissful, foolish moments, and they said " Good night " indeed.

She went to bed full of bright dreams of to-morrow : but who shall tell what to-morrow may bring forth ?

CHAPTER XIX.

CLARICE sat at her toilet-table the next morning, looking earnestly on her own reflection in the glass. It was not often she indulged in this feminine weakness— though it is not exclusively feminine either, for I have seen elderly men gaze upon their own elderly faces, twizzle their moustaches, caress their grey beards, and arrange their scanty grey locks, with the self-satisfaction— to use the mildest term—of a girl in her teens preparing for her first ball.

Clarice did not care to look at herself as a rule, for sometimes something she dreaded

seemed to look back at her out of her own
eyes, that made her shiver and turn away ;
but now she regarded herself with some
curiosity, wondering and trying to see what
his eyes saw in her face. But it was no
use ; she could not tell—her own face swam
in the mirror for a moment, and then faded
from it, and *his* brown eyes smiled back
at her. Thus her effort at self-inspection
was a failure. Others might have found a
wondrous charm in the picture the mirror
presented : a fair - complexioned woman,
with a mass of golden hair tumbling in
billowy waves about her shoulders and
rippling daintily over the low white brow,
forming a glorious setting to the lovely face
now eloquent with its first love's sweet
mystery. It seemed as though some holy
fire had been kindled within her, and
rushed through her veins and set every
fibre quivering, and transfigured her with a

strange new beauty. Her face was aglow
with a glad, happy light. But she found
no pleasure in the contemplation of her
own charms; she turned away, and looked
from the window upon the scene they two
had trod together last night.

It was a lovely day, and the wild wide
landscape was well worth looking at. The
sky had shed a few rainy tears during the
night, and they fell on shrubs and grass
and flowers, sparkling like diamonds, till the
sun rose lazily, as though he didn't care to
be awakened so early, and thirstily drank
them up; and the green earth looked all the
fresher and greener for the showery visi-
tation. The tall trees shook out and
rustled their leafy branches, as if preening
themselves for the great day's beauty; the
lovely flowers opened their meek eyes shyly,
sighing their sweet fragrance to the wandering breeze, while the statelier blooms

opened their passionate hearts, fold by fold,
to be kissed by every wind that blew ; and
the sea, the grand old sea that had lain
shrouded and silent through the night,
threw off her grey veil, burst into rippling
waves of laughter, tossing her foamy arms
aloft, and was already coquetting with the
morning sun.

All this Clarice saw and felt keenly ; she
had never looked upon the familiar landscape with such eyes as she looked upon it
now ; every feature seemed new and strange
to her, as though glorified by the breath of
a new divinity. So true it is that we make
for ourselves the world around us, and see
with the eyes of the spirit rather than the
eyes of the flesh. That which to one is
but a tame, commonplace prospect, to
another, flooded with the sunshine of hope
and memory, is clothed with supreme
loveliness. Her whole nature seemed to

be in unison with the world around; she felt that she was a part of *it*, as *it* was a part of her. Her pulse throbbed with the throbbing of the great sea, and her heart, overflowing with its new-born joy, seemed full, and swooning with the perfume of the flowers.

As she progressed slowly with her toilette, the very room seemed alive with airy tongues that spoke to her spirit's ear in a language that words would be inadequate to translate. Mere words are poor things when needed for the illustration of deep feeling, whether of joy or sorrow; everybody has felt that who has ever felt at all.

However, we must come down from the most beatified condition of bliss to face this everyday and commonplace world, that still keeps the even tenour of its ways. Joy-bells may be ringing or a funeral dirge be tolled, hearts may be swelling with joy or breaking

with sorrow, empires may fall and kings lie
low in the dust, starving souls may shrivel
in their miserable mortal frames—but the
body has a digestion : it gets hungry ; as a
mere matter of mechanism it gets vulgarly
hungry, and it must be fed ; feeding time
for the whole human race comes round as
regularly as the sun rises and sets. So it
happened that Clarice was recalled to take
up the burden of everyday life by the sound
of Miriam's voice at the door, telling her
that the breakfast-bell had rung ten
minutes ago. Then she threw open the
door, and stood upon the threshold like a
radiant vision—

> " In glory of gold and glory of hair,
> And glory of glorious face most fair."

Miriam looked in her face, kissed her, and
knew—and was glad. She had a generally
haunting idea that her " dear Clarice " lay

near to Jack Swayne's heart; the idea was not a pleasant one, as it kept her, Miriam, beyond the pale of possibilities—for she loved Jack herself very dearly, very devoutly, though in a practical way. It was love, all the same, though of a different quality, and blended with thoughts of bonnets and butcher's bills, and other practical necessities of this life, which romantic folk are in the habit of ignoring. Of course Jack's handsome person occupied the foreground—the rest were grouped round as mere accessories, but they were necessary to make the whole complete.

People have different ways of loving: some are of the earth—earthy; some are lifted to a higher atmosphere altogether, and reach nearer heaven, where love is spiritual and complete. These combine the ideal with the real, and revel in the delicate refinements of the affections; they feel more keenly and enjoy more. But one can't blame the earthern pitcher for not being Dresden china ; and, after all, a good commonplace, everyday affection, warranted to wear well, satisfies most men. Fortunately in the world of the affections each can ally himself—or at least propose the alliance—to that nature which suits his own ; can choose his counterpart or his opposite, as he pleases. Metaphorically speaking, one man "embarks his soul in a kiss," and revels in an atmosphere of sentiment and emotional pleasures ; another will find his bliss in a well-cooked chop or savoury stew : and who shall say which is wisest and best ? Each judges for himself.

Well, Clarice and Miriam, each with her heart closed upon her own secret, joined Mr. Fleming at the breakfast-table. They found him deeply occupied with his morning's mail—so much so that he scarcely noticed their entrance; he merely glanced up and mechanically wished them "good morning," then with bent brows returned to his correspondence. Clarice asked no questions, made no remark; with servants in the room and a guest at table, it was no time for confidential conversation. Clarice felt vexed that anything should happen to worry him on this day when "Hugh was coming!" When she handed him his coffee he laid aside his letters, and entered into the general chit-chat which enlivened their morning meal. As soon as it was over, and nobody seemed inclined to linger, they rose up and went their several ways. Clarice followed Mr. Fleming to his study.

"What is it, father dear?" she asked; "something troubles you, I know."

"Well, yes, my dear child," he answered, "I am rather worried; I have received some unpleasant communication from my Paris

bankers; they are in something of a dilemma, and don't seem inclined to act
without first having a personal consultation
and instruction from me. I must run over
at once and see exactly how matters stand.
Of course I am the only person who can
take the responsibility of acting. Just give
me Bradshaw, my dear. I think I may
manage to catch the tidal train for Boulogne
and Paris to-night. Let me see—yes," he
added, running his eye down the compli-
cated page, " train leaves Penally at 11
o'clock, reaches Paddington at 8.10. Tidal
train starts at 9.25 to-night, so I can
catch it without any hurry; there is still an
hour before we need start. You will go
with me, Clary? the trip will do you good."

" *I* go with you *to-day!*" exclaimed
Clarice, blankly. " Oh, darling dad, I cannot—it is impossible!"

" Why? why impossible?" he exclaimed,

surprised at her hesitation; for as a rule she would not let him stir without her, and sometimes insisted on accompanying him at a great inconvenience. "There, run away, dress, and come along; we shall only be away a few days, and Katrina can put up the little you want in five minutes."

"But, dad dear, I could not possibly go to-day—and I am sorry you've got to go. I—I wanted to talk to you about something."

"Well, my dear, if you really *won't* go, you must bottle up that something till I come back; I dare say it will keep without spoiling. But I really don't see why you can't go with me—then we could discuss the 'something' as we go along." Clarice was struck with a bright thought.

"Why, there is Miriam, Papa; you have forgotten her. I could not possibly turn her out of doors, could I ? "

" Humph—well, perhaps not," he admitted reluctantly; " but there, we mustn't stand chattering—we're wasting time. I must post up my papers. Run away, put on your hat, and drive with me to the station."

His masculine preparation did not take long to make; he was soon equipped in light marching order, a valise and an umbrella answering all his requirements.

The two girls drove with him to the station; they were in plenty of time, and took a few turns up and down the platform before the train came up.

" God bless you, my little girl! " he exclaimed, at parting; " I can't bear to leave you. Take care of yourselves and be happy. I wish I could send Jack down to look after you, but he can't leave London just yet."

As the train steamed off—they watched

it till it was out of sight—Clarice's heart sank; for the moment she wished she had thrown everything else aside and gone with him.

They stopped at the Rectory on their way homeward to have a chat with Mrs. Spencer. She was surprised to see them at that unusual hour, but they explained that they had been seeing Mr. Fleming off by the train, and were going to have the Manor House all to themselves for the next few days. She at once saw an opportunity for improving their minds, and giving them the benefit of her society for a longer period than was usual during their social visitings. She wanted to visit some poor people in their neighbourhood, she said; so she would kill two birds with one stone, and spend a nice long day at the Manor House. "Pity we can't have a Dorcas meeting, my dear Clarice," she exclaimed, always ready to

improve a situation, " but there's no time to
arrange that; and, my dear, if it will not
inconvenience you very much, the Rector
shall fetch me home in the evening. I will
not trouble you for the carriage," she added,
magnanimously, " he shall drive over in the
pony chaise; and it will be a capital opportunity for him to see your dear father's
improvement in the way of warming the
conservatory, which I believe is on an en-
tirely new principle."

Thus cornered, the exigencies of civiliza-
tion compelled Clarice to play the hypocrite
in a small way. She was obliged to *seem*
gratified by the proposal, and to suggest
that the Rector should dine at the Manor
House; she could not well have done other-
wise.

Mrs. Spencer received the invitation with
such evident satisfaction, that the end of
her nose seemed to sharpen and grow redder

than ever as by rapid calculation she set
"one day off the house bill." She kept
the girls waiting while she rushed to the
kitchen to counterorder her meagre instructions, to give an extra screw to the larder
and a squeeze to the cook's conscience;
then dashed into the Rector's study, where
he was busily engaged writing a sermon on
extra vigorous principles. He felt that his
flock failed to realize in its full strength the
absolute personality of the devil, so he tried
to paint him in all the horrors of brimstone
and fire, and meant to make him the figure-
head of his next Sunday's discourse. If that
didn't frighten people into the right way,
nothing would! To his thinking, fear, not
love, was the great virtue-conductor, and he
did his best to cultivate that to its highest
extent. He did not take his eight hundred
a year for nothing: he did his best for his
flock, and gave them all the light he

possessed — it might be but a farthing rushlight; but such as it was he gave it liberally. He was so dazed with his own eloquence, that he could hardly receive the fact that he was expected to dine at the Manor House at seven o'clock that evening.

Mrs. Spencer was soon ready, and the trio started on their way to the Manor House, conversing in the most lively fashion. She always prided herself on her agreeability, and was even more agreeable than usual. But Clarice, who had looked forward to a very different manner of passing the day, could scarcely hide her chagrin; and when Hugh came in later in the day, plumed with hope and brimming over with happy expectations, and found his female parent in full and proud possession of the field where he had hoped to exercise the whole army of his affections, and to carry on operations during the whole day within the limits of the love lines, his feelings may be better imagined than described. I should be sorry to translate his inward anathemas into plain phrases, but he bore his disappointment bravely, and made himself the life of the party; and the day passed more pleasantly than perhaps, under the circumstances, could have been expected.

They strolled about the gardens and through the greenhouses, Mrs. Spencer begging "just a little cutting" from everything she saw. She contrived to make prying excursions to sundry nooks and corners of the old Manor House; her curiosity burrowed into all kinds of forbidden places; she threw her fishing-line freely on all sides, and fished persistently—but caught nothing; and actually with great cunning fished Katrina, with whom she held quite a long suggestive conversa-

tion—but she might as well have fished a
a marble monument! However, on the
whole she had a very pleasant time, and
though she deplored the extravagance of
the dinner table, she enjoyed it nevertheless.   It is quite a different matter to
indulge at another person's expense than at
our own.   She openly regretted that she
could not take up her quarters at the Manor
House during Mr. Fleming's absence, that
Clarice might have the benefit of her
superintending genius; but as that was
impossible, she promised to spend a great
portion of every day there.   They drove
back to the Rectory soon after dinner ; but
Hugh stayed on for an hour to hear all the
news from Clarice's lips, and take his
reward for his long day's abstinence.   It
was a dull, dreary evening; there was neither
moon nor stars, and a drizzling rain was
falling, but they cared nothing for the

weather, and might have echoed the
words—

"On all this dusk and gloom and light
The moon may rise or not to-night;
But in my soul she rises bright."

In consideration of the proprieties of life,
Hugh left much earlier than he would
have done if the master of the house had
been at home. Clarice had carried the
Bradshaw about all day, and followed Mr.
Fleming through all the stages of his
journey.

"To-morrow at eleven o'clock he will
reach Paris," she said. "The dear old dad!
he will be travelling while we are asleep in
our beds."

"You girls don't mind being alone in the
house? You are sure you don't feel timid
or nervous?" observed Hugh.

"I'm never nervous," exclaimed Miriam,
virtuously; "I always feel we are in the
hands of Providence."

" But Providence does sometimes allow the ' burglar to go a burgling,' " suggested Hugh. " I'll mount guard outside if you like, and patrol with the vigilance of a sentinel all night."

Clarice laughed.

" I'm never nervous, either," she answered; " besides, I shall take father's derringer upstairs with me, and any marauder would have a warm reception."

But no marauder did come; the night passed peacefully, and the morning broke clear, cool, and bright. Hugh, determined not to be baulked that day, stole a march upon his parent, made his appearance on the scene quite early, and the trio improvised a picnic in the woods. Of course if Clarice had been alone this could not have been; but Miriam, his own sister, being on a visit there, made all the difference.

Mrs. Spencer timed her visit that day so that she might arrive just about the hour for luncheon, with an appetite sharpened by the drive, and heightened by a meagre breakfast; for it did not do to have too many good things on one day, so in anticipation of a dainty luncheon she had cut off her customary egg! She drove up to the house aglow with exercise and hunger. Lo! the birds had flown; nobody knew whither they had gone, but they were not expected home till the day was over! Here was a blow! But there was no help for it; disappointed and crestfallen she was compelled to return home and revenge herself on an empty larder!

With the young people all went well: they lounged through the sunshiny hours in a paradise of their own making; then they spread their luncheon under the trees, and laughed and chatted in a happy, foolish

way. As for Clarice, she had never dreamed
that such golden moments could gather on
the sands of time ! Hugh's fresh, breezy
voice invigorated and acted upon her like a
tonic ; his smile sent sunshine to her heart
and made her strong and glad ! To-day
was to-day; she had no thought of to-
morrow, or of any to-morrow that might
follow it—eternity was lost in the *now !*
She had not had enough experience of life
to have any foreshadowing, or to realize
the fact that, so sure as night follows day,
our brightest moments are flying fast to
join the past days and hours that have died
in mist and pain; that joy, being briefer
than sorrow, has swifter wings, flies faster,
and—is gone !

For young, happy souls, "sufficient for
the day is the evil thereof." This day
closed as happily as it began. It was one
to be marked with a white stone !—there

are none too many such in any lives. Some look back over a dead level plain, and find the black or the grey stones outnumber the white by a hundred to one!

The next morning the Manor House was thrown into a state of confusion by a bomb-shell falling on the breakfast-table in the shape of a telegram, which ran thus—

"CONTINENTAL HOTEL, PARIS.

"*Messrs. Drewett and Co. to Miss Lemaire.*

"Mr. Fleming taken seriously ill. Come at once. Messenger will meet you at Paddington Station. Take 11 o'clock train."

Here was a blow to poor Clarice! Love, hope, joy—all was forgotten, merged in the one terrible thought that *he* was struck down, perhaps dying, and she so many hundred miles away! She reproached herself bitterly for not having gone with him. In a state of utter distraction she flew to Katrina, and told her with sobs and hysterical emotion what had happened. Katrina realized the necessity for prompt action, and proceeded with trembling hands to put together such things as were necessary for the journey. Clarice would have flung on her hat and dashed off at once; but Miriam, who always had her wits about her, and was not to be overcome by another's distress (nor indeed overmuch by her own, for if she had been at her last gasp she would have given instructions to the undertaker, and been special in her orders for the fashion of her shroud!) came to the rescue now.

"It is no use going before the train starts," she exclaimed, practically, "and that will not be for another hour yet. Come, Clarice dear, you must take a little coffee. You know you want to be a help and comfort to him; if you don't take care of yourself you will be neither. If you go on like this you will be exhausted when you get there, and I should not wonder if the doctors forbid your seeing him at all."

Clarice quite realized the truth of Miriam's position, and pulled herself together as well as she could. She stifled her sobs and slowly dried her tears ; but it is difficult, when we are shaken by a storm of deep feeling, sorrow blind and heart-aching, to lift ourselves to the level of good, simple common sense. Still Clarice grew calm with the necessity for calmness. She thought of Jack, and felt that he ought to be communicated with. She was too agitated to write ; so she sent the telegram to him at once—that would tell him all that he would need to know.

She and Katrina started by the same train which had carried Mr. Fleming away two days before.

CHAPTER XX.

CHECKMATE !

THEY reached Paddington late in the evening. The station lamps were lighted, and one huge globe of electric light shone down like a full moon, throwing a white radiance everywhere. It seemed to be the busiest hour of the day, so great was the stir and bustle on all sides. An excursion train had just come in, and was emptying its animated freight upon the platform ; porters were trundling their laden trucks, and " b'y'r-leave " seemed echoing through the air like the song of the mocking-bird. Long serpentine trains came slowly

creeping in and out; engines whistled and
snorted, filling the air with discordant
shrieks and yells, as though a score of
demons had been let loose from below and
were trying to find their way back again;
while the grimed faces of firemen and
stokers glowed in the smoke and flame of
the engine fire—making in all a weird, wild
scene to unaccustomed eyes.

The many coloured lights, the noise, the
babel of tongues, and moving masses of
people, were all to Katrina brain-bewilder-
ing. The question suggested itself, " Who
was to meet them? and how could they
possibly be recognized amid such a moving
multitude?" Clarice, also anxious, hesitated before descending to the platform, and
stood in the doorway gazing eagerly round.
Katrina no less eagerly looked over her
shoulder. Meanwhile a dignified official
was pacing leisurely down the platform

beside the carriages, and glancing into each
compartment with the brief inquiry, "Any
one named Lemaire here?" Clarice caught
the sound of her own name; Katrina, behind
her, being for the moment too bewildered
by the confusion of sounds to distinguish
anything distinctly.

"Here! here!" exclaimed Clarice, re-
sponding quickly. "Quick, Katrina! here's
somebody for us." The words were flung
over her shoulder for Katrina to catch them,
as Clarice sprang out of the carriage.
Before she had time to think or look round,
she felt her arm lightly seized, and a soft
voice said in a low tone—

"Miss Lemaire, I believe? This way,
please; my servant will attend to your
maid."

Clarice, with momentary hesitation,
glanced back, and saw Katrina, loaded with
hand baggage, being assisted by some one

as she cautiously descended from the carriage. " So it was all right so far ; " in another moment she was being guided by her escort through the crowd, towards a carriage that waited at one of the station doors. As soon as Katrina found herself safely standing on the platform, she glanced to where Clarice had stood a moment before. But she was no longer there! she had disappeared as if by magic. Katrina glanced round in some alarm in search of her ; soon her dazed eyes caught sight of the girlish figure of her young mistress, already some distance off among the crowd, while beside her, and towering above her, was the grey head and smiling face of M. Lemaire.

Although a conflicting mass of people surged between them, she plunged into their midst with a smothered exclamation, and tried to fight her way through to reach those who were fast disappearing in the distance ; but the more she struggled the more her progress was impeded. At last, in desperation, she appealed to those around her. She might as well have appealed to a tombstone.

" For God's sake ! stop him ! stop her ! " she exclaimed, breathlessly. But who cares for a stranger's distress ? However kindly disposed individuals may be, a crowd is always cruel. Some laughed, some regarded her with cool *sang froid* and passed on ; others eyed her curiously. Everybody was indifferent—nobody cared ! One wag, with a broad grin at grey hairs in distress, called out—

" Ease her ! Stop her ! Don't you see the old lady's after the steam-engine ! "

" Stop him ! " she exclaimed, as the policeman came up.

" Stop who, ma'am—have you lost any-thing ? "

" No, no! " she exclaimed, the official inquiry reducing her agitated nerves to a state
of order. After all, what could she say?
how explain her dilemma? If she did, how
could a stranger comprehend it? Besides,
what right had she to expose family secrets
outside the family circle? She would do
nothing on her own responsibility. She
must wait and think. The officer saw her
agitation, and did not increase it by observation or remarks, but waited patiently for
her to speak—which she did as soon as
she had sufficiently collected her thoughts.
" No," she said, " she had lost nothing;
only she had just come up from the country
and had missed her young lady."

" Oh! if that's all I advise you to go into
the waiting-room; I dare say she'll come
back to look for you." He showed her to
the waiting-room and there left her, adding,
" I'll go and have a look round; if she's as

anxious to find *you* as you are to find *her*, I
shall meet her looking about somewhere
outside." He lounged off and left her to
herself. She pondered for awhile. What
had she better do ? She knew the name of
the firm of Mr. Fleming's solicitors, but it
was too late to expect to find them—their
office would be closed. Then there was
Mr. Swayne ; she did not know whether he
was in London: if he were, of course he was
the fittest person to be communicated with.
She racked her brain trying to remember
his address. She had often put letters in
the postbag for him, but on the spur of the
moment could not remember the direction.
She knew it was the name of an animal—
" Fox Court," " Lamb Street." No. She
had it at last—it was " Hare Court ! " Now
where was Hare Court ?

She got into a cab—that suggested itself
as the wisest thing to do, and directed the

man to drive to Hare Court as quickly as
possible. In the course of a few minutes he
stopped at the quaint little gateway in Fleet
Street, and here he put her down, telling
her to " apply to the gentleman with the
gold-laced hatband for any information she
wanted." To the gold-laced hatband she
accordingly applied, and learned from him
all she wished to know. " Yes, Mr. Swayne
was in London, and occupied his rooms in
Hare Court. He directed her most courteously where she was to go. He could
not leave his post, or he would show her the
way, but she could not possibly miss it—just
past the church on the right-hand side."

As she turned out of Fleet Street, with its
glare of light and tramping multitudes, into
the silent solitude of the Temple, she felt
oppressed, as though she was entering a new
world. There was no one about, and the tall,
grim buildings were silhouetted against the

dark-blue sky; the tread of her own footsteps jarred upon her ears. It was so quiet, so lonely, she could hardly believe she was so near the living world of men and women. The sound of the roaring tide of life, that was streaming on like the rush of a mighty river, followed her, like the smothered roll of a muffled drum broken into a thousand ghostly echoes. The old church, with its many-centuried monuments of the heroic dead, loomed gloomily on her left; and on her right, in a kind of quadrangle, were a few tall, dingy-looking, dimly-lighted buildings. She mounted the steps of one, and running her eye down the list of names found the one she wanted—" Mr. Swayne, first floor."

It was all plain-sailing now ! With alacrity she ascended the narrow worm-eaten stairs, and on the first door to the right she again read his name, painted in big white ugly letters on a massive old door, so heavy, dark, and frowning, it looked as though it would never allow itself to be opened. But it was opened, and that speedily, in answer to her modest tinkle of a tiny bell; and Jack, with a smart gold-tasselled smoking-cap on his head, and a flowing dressing-gown clothing his stalwart limbs, a meerschaum between his lips, stood in the aperture. He stared at Katrina blankly for a moment. He never allowed himself to be taken by surprise. " He never was surprised at anything," he used to say— and so far had never been thrown off his balance in his life !

" Hullo, Katrina ! " he exclaimed, genially, " what's up ? Something, or you wouldn't be here."

" You—you haven't got Miss Clarice's letter yet ? " returned Katrina, scarcely knowing where to begin.

"No; haven't heard from her for a week. Why?"

"You know your uncle went to Paris three days ago?"

"The devil he did!" ejaculated Jack. "I knew nothing about it. Go on."

"Things went on very pleasantly at first," she continued, "as Miss Miriam is staying at the Manor House, and Mr. Hugh came every day and kept the young ladies lively—he's just the sort of gentleman to do that. And—this morning——Oh dear! how agitated I am; I hardly know how to go on."

"Well, fire away!" exclaimed Jack, impatiently; "you haven't come all this way to expatiate on Mr. Hugh's powers of 'keeping the young ladies lively.'"

"I am 'firing away,' sir, as fast as I can," she answered, in accents of mild reproach. "I always think it's right to begin at the beginning of things if you want to be thoroughly understood. If I was to tell you that Miss Clarice had gone off with M. Lemaire, you'd want to know all about it."

"In the name of seven devils! what do you mean?" thundered Jack, and down went the meerschaum with a crash.

"That's just where I was coming to. This morning Miss Clarice got a telegram saying that Mr. Fleming was seriously ill at some hotel in Paris, and she was to come directly, and a messenger would meet her at Paddington railway station——"

"Who sent the telegram? Was my uncle able to do it?"

"I think the telegram was from the bankers," she answered; "and we came off by the first train this morning. At the station there were such crowds, such confusion, that while I was getting the things together I lost Miss Clarice, and when I looked round I saw her a long way off, being hurried through the crowd by M. Lemaire. So she's lost, sir!—he has got her!—and what are we to do?"

Having got to the end of her story, the old woman relapsed into a state of agitation, and began rocking herself to and fro and moaning fragmentary snatches of distress.

Jack glared at her angrily, but he answered coolly and tersely—

"We must find her, of course, and get her out of his clutches as soon as we can. There, it's no use making a hullabaloo—we want cool heads." He glanced at the clock as though he was expecting somebody, and paced up and down the room like a caged animal that couldn't get out. "What the devil is Wagstaff about?" he exclaimed, grinding his teeth impatiently. Then he flung the outer door wide open and listened; presently he heard a step he knew upon the stairs, and in another moment the expected Wagstaff stood on the landing. Jack hurried forward to meet him.

"Come in, Wagstaff, come in! Well, what news? You've got some, I know."

"Right you are, sir," replied Wagstaff, nodding his head. "I have got a scrap or two, and you shall have it right off. I told you yesterday that *he* "—jerking his head as though Jack must understand who was meant by the emphatic *he*—"had taken two berths aboard the Anchor Line steamer, *City of Rome.*"

"And I thought we should be rid of him, and you would have ended your labours," observed Jack. "Well, go on."

"Exactly, that's so, sir—except that our labours are never ended. When we finish at one end, we begin at the other. But that's neither here nor there. To-day he's been very busy writing letters and doing a little shopping in the tailoring line. This evening he went to the Paddington station and waited until the express train from Cornwall arrived. There he met a handsome young lady——"

" So far I know," exclaimed Jack, eagerly. " You did not lose sight of him ? "

" Not likely," replied Wagstaff, receiving the insinuation of such a possibility as a professional insult. " They got into a carriage—I followed in a hansom ; they drove to the Blackfriars Hotel, and there they are now. They sail for America to-morrow on the *City of Rome.*"

" Sail for America to-morrow, do they ? " exclaimed Jack, rubbing his hands gleefully together. " I rather think not ! I mean to take a hand at that little game. Katrina, make yourself at home. I'm off ! "

" You'll allow me to go with you, sir ? "

said Wagstaff; "in case of any little difficulty, you know, I might be useful."

Jack accepted his offered companionship, and the two left Hare Court together.

And how did it fare with Clarice? She had hardly time to think, let alone to speak, as she was being hurried through the crowd. When she found herself seated in the carriage with her venerable escort beside her, she glanced anxiously in his face and inquired—

"My father—when did you leave him? Is he better?"

"Much better," he replied, frankly. "A change for the better took place within an hour after the telegram had been sent off, and when I left him all cause for serious anxiety was over."

"Thank God!" she exclaimed, with a sigh of relief, as she leaned back in the carriage more content. Conversation could not very well be carried on as they rattled through the streets. Occasionally she glanced at the face of her father's messenger, momentarily lighted up as they flashed past the lamp-posts.

" Are you sure we are in time for the boat ? " she inquired, presently.

" Ay, the boat ! Well, there is a little difficulty about that," he answered; " but we shall see."

" What difficulty ? " she inquired. " Oh ! I hope nothing will prevent our crossing to-night ! We calculated we should be quite in time for the train."

" But, my dear young lady, things don't always fall out according to our calculations," he answered; " and as your train happened to be late in arriving, and the tidal train starts nearly an hour earlier to-night, I am afraid you have just managed to—miss it."

This communication threw Clarice into a great state of agitation and distress, and he did his best to calm her.

" Remember, your father trusted you in my charge, and I have already made all arrangements for you to be properly cared for. The delay is but for a few hours, as we start quite early in the morning."

" You are very kind," murmured Clarice, disconsolately. " And where is Katrina ? Does she know ? "

" No doubt my servant will have informed her by this time."

The carriage now stopped at a hotel in a busy, bustling thoroughfare. He was most attentive, and assisted her to alight, and escorted her to a cosy room on the first floor, which had evidently been prepared for her reception. The gas was lighted, and a bright wood-fire was blazing in the grate— for it was a damp evening, and the fire was pleasant to look at, if not necessary for warmth. Everything had been done for her comfort ; she could not but feel grateful, and she tried to look gratefully appreciative : that was a more difficult task, for it was very sad and lonely to be there in a strange place, in a stranger's care, with no familiar face near, no one to speak to. He assisted her in taking off her things, wheeled an easy-chair to the fireside.

"Thank you, I would rather look out of the window," she said ; " and will you please send Katrina to me as soon as she comes ? "

Of course he promised to do so, and showed her a little adjoining room in which she was to sleep.

" And I hope you will sleep well, for you will have to be up early in the morn-ing."

" I shall not try to sleep—I only want

the morning to come. Do you think it will be long before my maid arrives ?"

"All in good time ; and I do hope, as your father's friend, you will rest content in my hands, and for the time being regard me as a father indeed. Would that be very difficult ?" And he laid his hand with fatherly tenderness upon her head.

"Oh no ! no !" she exclaimed ; "you are very good to me, but I am so—so disappointed ! "

She turned her head away, for a lump was rising in her throat, and the tears would gather in her eyes. For the moment a little dramatic scene presented itself to his mind. He was half inclined to clasp her to his heart—at least to his waistcoat— and claim her "his darling—his long-lost child ! " at once. But the impulse of the moment passed. It would not be wise to add still greater agitation to her mind in its present state. He would bide his time, and not risk all until she was more thoroughly isolated from old associations. He did not know how far she had been informed of her own history, nor in what light she had been taught to regard him. He must try to find out; but there was time enough for that.

He had mentally arranged his course of action, and had little doubt of the result. He would be able to manage her according to his desires; he had known how to cow and control stronger natures than hers. If she should prove troublesome—well, he had only to lament that his unfortunate child— ahem! nobody would take the trouble to interfere with him.

He ordered some light refreshment to be sent up; and, just to satisfy him, she took a few spoonfuls. Then he left her looking out upon the lighted streets, while he went

to finish up his little preparations for the
morning. He would look in again, he said,
in about an hour; that would be before she
retired to rest.

Left alone, she felt very sad and in some
perplexity, wondering about Katrina. It
was so odd that she had not yet arrived.
She sat there thinking and looking out,
watching the crowds go by, surging up and
down from all directions, for half a dozen
brilliantly lighted thoroughfares converged
upon her point of view. She had not been
seated there very long—though to her it
it seemed ages, time passed so slowly—
when the door opened and Jack Swayne
entered the room. A great wave of joy
surged up within her at sight of him; but
as she rose up with outstretched arms to
greet him, she only said—

"Oh, Jack, isn't it a pity we missed the
train?" It did not strike her as being at
all strange that he should be there.

"Yes, it is a pity," said Jack, tersely; "but put on your things and come with me at once."

"But, Jack, I can't do that!" she answered; "father has sent some one to meet me—he has only gone away for half an hour. I can't leave till he comes back; it would look so rude, so ungrateful, when he has been so kind to me."

"I'll make that all right," said Jack; "trust to me, and come quickly. Katrina's at my place waiting for you."

"Katrina at your place?" she exclaimed, opening her eyes wide with wonder; "why how strangely things are happening to-day!"

"Very strangely," repeated Jack; "but make haste; we can talk as we go along— we are wasting time."

She was accustomed to obey Jack, and she obeyed him now. She wanted to write a note of explanation to her father's messenger. But she couldn't, as she did not know his name. However, in order that she should be quite content, Jack went into the hotel office and scribbled a message for him.

He took her straight to his rooms in Hare Court, where Katrina had contrived that everything should look homely and pleasant to her. Clarice was delighted; it was no use telling her to be quiet—she would know how Katrina came there.

"Well, my dear," she answered, simply— as, having received no instructions from Jack, she left him to make the important communication—"I only just turned my back for a moment, when I lost you, and could not find which way you had gone. It was very awkward, and I thought the best thing I could do was to come on here."

"But that is very strange," said Clarice,

with puckered brows. "I wasn't lost at all! I went with the gentleman father had sent, as he promised, to meet us; I saw you being helped out of the carriage, and he said his servant had orders to look after you, and bring you after us. I don't understand it; it is very strange, very mysterious. There must be a mistake, a misunderstanding, somewhere.

She paused a moment. Nobody spoke. Turning to Jack suddenly she exclaimed—

"Why, Jack, *you* are looking gloomy and mysterious now! What is it all about? What does it mean? I know there is something to tell — what is it?" Struck by a sudden dread, she cried in a voice sharpened by anxiety, "Oh, Jack! is it anything about father? Have you heard? Is he *worse?*"

Jack's face reassured her before he spoke.

"Make yourself quite easy on that point," he said; " I don't believe there is anything the matter with my uncle."

"But how about the telegram, Jack?" exclaimed the bewildered girl; "see what it says." The message, which she had sent from Penally, had just been delivered, and lay on the table before her; she eagerly tore it open and showed it to him.

" That never came from my uncle at all," exclaimed Jack, decisively. Seeing that Clarice was excited now, he knew her well enough to know that she would be content with nothing less than the whole truth. " The fact is, dear, you have been inveigled up to London on false pretences, and were separated from Katrina by design, not accident! "

" By whose design? and why?" she exclaimed. " I think that could hardly be— you forget my father's messenger—— "

"Was no messenger at all," he inter-rupted her; "Katrina saw and recognized him! Clary dear, can you bear to hear it?—he was the man from whom we have tried to guard you all your life! He was M. Lemaire, the man whom the law recognizes as your father!"

All the light and life died out of her face. She stared at him, white and blank with terror, and clutched him fast.

"There is no cause for alarm now, dear," he added; "you are as safe here as though you were in Windsor Castle. Katrina, you must make her sleep."

"I could not sleep," she said, with a strange calmness. "Jack, don't go! Stay and talk—tell me all about it."

"There is no more to say, dear; you know everything. He lured you up to town by that false message; but I spoilt that little game, and it is all right now.

After such a day of excitement you must have rest. Don't think, don't worry; leave that part of the business to us. I shall be with you early in the morning."

Clarice was strangely silent after he had left them; she made no attempt to enter into conversation with Katrina — did not even make any remark on the strange incidents of the day. She was tired and worn-out; but whenever the anxious Katrina looked at her during the night, she found her with wide-open, wakeful eyes staring at the ceiling.

The next morning Jack arrived early and in good spirits. He had telegraphed to Mr. Fleming and brought his answer, which ran thus·—

" Hôtel Continental, Paris.

"Am quite well. Have never been ill. Return home to-morrow."

END OF VOL. II.